DUCHESS OF SEDUCTION

BEVERLEY OAKLEY

SANI
PUBLISHING

CHAPTER 1

"The Earl of Lovett has taken a mistress?"

The breathy shock of pretty newlywed, Mrs. Rupert Browne, sliced through the buzz of conversation, lancing its unsuspecting target three feet away and causing a deaf colonel to ask the duchess if she required a glass of water.

"Of all the men in this town, he was the last— Why, Catherine are you not astonished?"

Still choking on her champagne, Cressida, Lady Lovett, strained to hear the response of her cousin, Catherine, who had obviously disseminated the shocking *on dit* regarding her husband while she smilingly assured deaf Colonel Horvitt she was quite all right, as if her happiness were not suddenly hanging by a gossamer thread.

The colorful throng in the ballroom seemed to sway like jeering miasmas as Cressida clutched her shepherdess's crook, glad to have the foolish prop of her fancy dress costume provide such unexpected support.

She only hoped she was making the right responses to the colonel's monologue. Meanwhile, all her concentration was focused on the nearby conversation as she waited desperately for a rejection of the outrageous claim.

"Indeed! And yes, surely not?" gasped the generally well-intentioned but oblivious Mrs. Browne to Cousin Catherine's whispered reply. The two were in a huddle of black and gold silk and ermine, clearly enjoying the opportunity to dress as 17th century palace courtiers at tonight's lavish entertainment. "The earl made a love match. Mama told me he scandalized society by marrying a nobody. Why, that was but a handful of years ago."

Cressida had to use two hands to keep her champagne coupe steady. The indignity of being described as a 'nobody' was nothing compared with the pain of hearing her husband's amours—real or otherwise—discussed in the middle of a ballroom.

"Why, I remember the word around town was that he insisted that the state of his heart was of greater consequence than his pocket book. But that was then. I daresay after all those children—"

The children! How could anyone speak of her darlings like that? Cressida forced her trembling mouth into her best attempt at a smile as the colonel leaned forward and wagged his finger at her, his stentorian tone precluding further eavesdropping. "Your husband ruffled more than a few feathers with his speech in the House of Lords last night, Lady Lovett."

Cressida was in no mood for his bantering tone. Or for giggling as she'd once been in the habit of doing with her fearfully forceful but often entertaining cousin. Clearly, Cousin Catherine was disclosing details about the state of Cressida's marriage, of which Cressida, apparently, was the last to know. She straightened and pushed her shoulders back, suddenly self-conscious of appearing the sagging, lacking creature the several hundred guests crowded into Lady Belton's newly renovated ballroom must imagine her, if they were already privy to what she was hearing for the first time. Before her last sip of champagne, she'd considered herself happily married. It was all she could do to remain standing and dry-eyed.

Adjusting the lace of her masquerade costume, she managed, faintly, "Ah, Colonel, you know Lord Lovett and his good causes." She tried to make it sound like an endearment, but the axis of her world had become centered on ascertaining what other titbits about her marriage Catherine was divulging to Mrs. Browne.

The music swelled to a crashing crescendo, the end of which was punctuated by Mrs. Browne's shocked squeak, "Surely *that* is not the woman? Madame Zirelli? Was she not once Lord Grainger's mistress? No! His wife? He divorced her? And now she and Lord Lovett—?"

If Cressida hadn't been holding a champagne coupe, she'd have pressed her hands against her ears. If she hadn't been a lady, she'd have dashed the champagne coupe to the floor.

But she was a mother. It's why she hadn't wanted to come to Lady Belton's masquerade. Little Thomas was teething, but her darling husband Justin had been especially persuasive tonight, reminding her that it had been a long time since they'd been out in public, and that, yes, he knew Thomas was cutting a tooth, but there was nothing Cressida could do that Nurse Flora couldn't, just for a few hours that evening.

Seeing his handsome face smiling down at her had been more than she could resist. Especially since she could acquiesce and please him—without the dangers of being faced with his charm within the bedchamber.

Searching the ballroom for her Justin, she spied him talking to her friend, Annabelle Luscombe and a dark-haired Castilian looking young woman, near the supper table. His look was enquiring, as if he were hanging on Annabelle's every word. Cressida knew he would take equal interest if Annabelle were talking about her latest bonnet or about the Sedleywich Home for Orphans, of which Justin was patron and Annabelle on the committee.

A frisson of longing speared her. Justin had often gazed at her with such a look of interest when she'd first met him. So handsome, so determined. So sincere.

The thought that he'd made a special plea for her presence tonight purely in the interest of stilling wagging tongues was almost too terrible to consider.

A mistress? Her kind, beloved, faithful Justin?

As if he were conscious of her from across the room, Justin turned, his dark brown eyes kindling at the sight of her, the warmth of his smile spreading comfort like a woolen mantle. It radiated across the heated, perfumed distance that separated them and sent the blood tingling through her extremities. Cocooned in such safety—a public ballroom—she could admit to the extent to which he aroused her. Dear Lord, he looked like a handsome prince taken right out of the pages of a storybook, his brown, wavy hair brushed fashionably forward, topped with the laurel wreath required by his costume, his sideburns contouring his elegantly chiseled, high cheekbones.

Even after all these years of marriage her body responded as if she were a girl in the first throes of love.

Dressed like a stately Roman senator, Justin was the stuff of every swooning maiden's dreams, yet it was she, insignificant Miss Cressida Honeywell, daughter of a poor country parson, who had won his heart all those years ago.

She'd thought she still had it—had vowed she'd always keep it.

Rallying, she took a step forward, responding to the invitation implicit in her husband's eye, but the colonel began counseling Cressida on the dangers of Justin making speeches about orphans and sanitation when he could better rouse his audience in the Lords if he concerned himself with more important matters.

Cressida bit back her response. Like the docile, well bred woman she'd trained herself to become, she instead smiled politely at the colonel while her heart beat like a drum in response to the smouldering look she'd just exchanged with her husband. A look that was enough to all but dismiss her fears.

Exhaling with relief, she rewarded the colonel with such radiance that he, obviously regarding this as encouragement, closed the distance between them as he pursued his argument.

Cressida took a discreet step backwards though she pretended to be invested in the exchange with the elderly gentleman before her; meanwhile she slanted another secretive smile at Justin. He raised one eyebrow and his lips quirked as if he might blow at kiss in her direction before he gallantly attended to the hunchbacked Dowager Duchess of Trentham, whose eightieth birthday celebration this was.

Justin had the gift of making every woman feel the center of his especial interest. Clearly something must have been misconstrued...

And yet.

Awareness prickled through her—that she had for some time sensed all was not quite right.

"Very true, as always, colonel." She was adept at trotting out the required niceties. Her face and her body could speak the language required of her while her mind took its own journey.

And the journey it was now forced to take was not a comfortable one.

Justin, lately, had not been the contented husband of old. The recent bolstering she'd silently received from him faded upon this acknowledgement as she dwelt upon the altered tenor of their relationship. A relationship that had begun with such hope and passion.

The colonel was still speaking. Lord, he could intone forever and she'd somehow know how to nod and murmur and smile in a way that was eminently satisfying to him.

But Justin was not like that. He could see through platitudes. He'd seen through her the moment her responses no longer indicated the true state of her heart.

Cressida squeezed her right hand into a fist until her fingernails pierced the flesh of her palm while her lips curved into a smile of even greater parody.

When had it all changed? *Why* had it all changed? Surely Catherine's words were nothing more than evil gossip with not a jot of truth to them. Catherine had always been a trouble-maker. A fun cousin, to be sure, but a jealous, discontented one, ready to stir up trouble at the first opportunity, nevertheless.

"And this preoccupation with orphans when there are matters of governing that should take precedence." The colonel's whining monologue was accompanied by a great twitching of his mighty moustache. Fluffy and white like two rabbits' tails lying end to end. If Catherine had been here, they might have giggled over it like two school girls if only to strip the conversation of any seriousness. Cressida was often confronted by emphatic views she did not share but which she was given no chance to refute. She simply wasn't the kind of woman who used forceful words to indicate her feelings.

But there were other ways to ensure her wishes were acceded to.

Another frisson of discomfort snaked its way through her and she bit her lip as she continued to respond like a marionette to her undemanding audience. The colonel only required that she observe the niceties and give him a hearing. He didn't really care what she thought.

But Justin— She swallowed painfully. Justin had always cared what she thought.

Justin. Longing tore at her as she turned towards him once more. She wanted to pick up her skirts and run through the ballroom, pushing people out of her way before snatching at Justin's finely tailored coat sleeve. She wanted to beg him in an impassioned whisper to run out into the night with her. To press her body against his and twine her hands behind his neck while he kissed her senseless.

Senseless so she need not think of the consequences and she could again be the wife he needed and deserved.

"My husband believes governing means following a path that ensures justice even to orphans," she said softly.

Justin adored children. Didn't he? Of course he did.

Her mind felt suddenly fragmented as she tried to assimilate the current conversation with the the truncated exchanges she'd had with Justin over the past few months. The children. Her needs, their needs.

She swallowed uncomfortably.

Justin's needs.

She shook her head as if that might shake out the demons while she confronted the unpalatable truth.

Cressida knew her behavior had not been beyond reproach—that she had withdrawn and that understandably, Justin was confused.

It had been some time since they'd enjoyed cosy evenings side by side upon the sofa; affection and playfulness leading to passionate bedroom trysts. How wonderful those days had been.

But the repercussions. She'd not thought they'd weigh so heavily upon her. Joyfulness had been the natural consequence of giving birth to their first healthy child. A second child had cemented the family unit. A third in such a short time had been tiring but Justin had insisted a second nurse was hired so that Cressida could regain her health as quickly as possible.

The birth of Thomas—their fourth—had been especially difficult.

Cressida sucked in a difficult breath at the memory. She had nearly died. The pain had been like nothing she'd ever experienced and she'd wondered if she'd ever again feel like her body belonged to her as it once had.

Fortunately, she had healed but the fear remained. How could she ever go through that again?

Forcing aside her shame, she turned in the direction of her cousin and took advantage of a pause in the colonel's complaints to say, "Catherine? A minute, if you please?"

Nodding politely at the colonel, Cressida waylaid the stately, dark-haired young woman dressed as a siren as the colonel—thankfully—responded to his wife's perfunctory summons. With a little intake of breath and a stammered excuse, the recently gossiping Mrs. Browne slipped away while Cousin Catherine betrayed her guilt with a blush.

"Why, Cressy, I did not notice you. How long have you been standing there?"

"Long enough to wonder who Madame Zirelli might be and what she is to my husband," Cressida responded with uncharacteristic harshness.

Catherine's hand flew to her mouth. "Oh, Cressy," she gasped. "I had no idea you— I'm so sorry. But of course, it's only gossip. You know how quick people are to jump to conclusions." But her cheeks were flushed. She knew she was guilty of the charges Cressida made.

"Only gossip?" Cressida demanded. "Gossip which it seems I'm the last to know."

Catherine became brisk. "I hope you're not complaining, my dearest cousin, for we are not all as blessed as you with an indulgent husband. Behold Miss Hardwicke over there who is to marry the man beside her."

Cressida's gaze followed the finger Catherine stabbed forcefully in the direction of an thin, aged peer with grey hair and a stoop.

"Have you heard Miss Hardwick rail against life's unfairnesss? No, for everyone is depending upon her to retify the family's finances thanks to her unexpected marriage offer."

Cressida stared at the tight-lipped expression on the face of the young woman's groom-to-be, and shuddered.

"You're looking unwell, Cressy. I'll take you home. We'll have a nice, cozy chat in the carriage, shall we? I hadn't expected to see you out this evening, you've been hiding away so long."

Cressida was about to argue that she planned to return home with Justin when Catherine took her arm, saying breezily, "Don't trouble yourself over Justin. He's asked me to tell you he's off to White's with Roddy Johnson. He knew you were anxious to return home to little Thomas."

Was that grim satisfaction she saw on her cousin's face?

It wasn't until she'd gained the darkness of the vehicle that Cressida broke her tense silence. She could barely force out the words, but she would not have Catherine secretly gloating over something Cressida was apparently the last to know about.

"I'd thank you to tell me everything you told Mrs. Browne." Sinking back against the squabs of her husband's plush equipage, she hid her disquiet beneath a veneer of dignified anger. "If she is under the impression Justin has taken a mistress, you apparently did little to disabuse her of that notion, when I know very well it is not true. I'd like to know the source of your information."

Catherine shifted beside her, and although Cressida could not see her face, she could tell she was uncomfortable. "No need to get on your high ropes, Cressy," she muttered, and Cressida could imagine the proud, defiant tilt to Catherine's pointed chin as she defended her actions, just as she had done all through her impish childhood and spirited adolescence. "Like you say, I'm sure there's nothing to it."

Cressida was not about to assume her normally pliant role in order to appease her cousin. Not when her happiness was at stake, and not when it concerned her husband. He was her light, her moon. In steely tones, she asked, "I would like to know, Catherine, how you gained the impression Justin has taken a mistress." This was too important for the tears to which Cressida was sometimes prone, especially lately. With her back pressed stiffly against the carriage seat in the darkness, she felt, ironically, as if some of her own youthful confidence had returned. Justin was the axis of her existence. If her happiness was at risk—though she was sure it was not—she needed to know so she could act.

"Justin appears just as loving toward you as he ever did, my dear," Catherine hedged. "Why, only last week when James and I dined with you, he remarked to me—"

"Obviously, you must have heard something specific. I'm sure you'd not repeat hurtful gossip."

"Really, Cressida, I think you are making too much of this." Catherine halted in the middle of her response, paused, then added in clipped tones, as if she were angry with her cousin, "All right then, if you must know, and since you've all but accused me of being a gossiping jade—though I had hoped to spare you—I'll tell you what whispers are buzzing around the salons in London."

In the gloom, her expression was combative. "Justin has been a regular visitor to Mrs. Plumb's Wednesday salons." She gave a self-righteous sniff. "And if you've never heard of her, James says Mrs. Plumb is an actress with literary pretensions. A very vulgar woman, I believe, who paints her face."

Now was not the time to remind Catherine that she herself was not averse to resorting to artifice to enhance her natural charms. Cressida gripped her reticule with trembling fingers and stared fiercely at her cousin. "I take it this Madame Zirelli is also a regular at Mrs. Plumb's. Is it on this flimsy basis that the rumors are circulating regarding Justin's...extramarital amours?" Hurt and anger banished Cressida's propensity to soften life's harsh realities. She rarely spoke so directly to anyone—certainly not to Catherine, who'd taunted Cressida since they'd been children for being 'churchyard poor', but whose respect Cressida had thought she'd gained through her glittering match with Justin. Now, Catherine had seized on the first opportunity to knock Cressida down to size. With dignity, she asked her cousin, "On what grounds am I to believe this? Come, Catherine, it is not like you to be anything but direct."

"If you prefer directness, Cressida," Catherine responded with an air of injury, "do you not think it perfectly reasonable that Justin, like most men after eight years of marriage, feels the need to seek diversion? Is it not perfectly understandable that after so long, you are no longer everything to him? What woman ever is?" she added bitterly.

Cressida gasped as if she had been struck, but her cousin went on, her green eyes glittering as the carriage passed beneath a lamp-post. "He is no different from every other man, but you fail to consider your good fortune, Cressy, for at least Justin is discreet."

"How can you say that?" Deflated, Cressida slumped into the

corner, glad of the dimness so she could hurriedly wipe away her tears. Catherine would enjoy her weakness. "You speak as if I am the last to know and that I've brought this upon myself. How would you feel if James—" A sudden illumination stopped her mid-sentence, and she put out her hand, saying before she could stop herself, "James has strayed again? Oh, Catherine, I'm so sorry."

"Save your sympathy for yourself, Cressy." Catherine drew away, as if Cressida's outstretched hand were as welcome as a snake. "I was under no illusions as to James' likely fidelity from the day we wed. He was always too handsome for me—you remember we overheard Mrs. Dooley saying it at our engagement ball?"

Cressida knew Catherine's wounding had been close to mortal all those years ago. Six, she recalled, wondering if by Catherine's calculations, Cressida should consider herself lucky for having retained her husband's loyalty for this long.

Shrugging, as if the matter were no longer of importance, Catherine went on, "James and now Justin are simply conforming to the prescribed role of husbands by doing what society condones within the limits of money and discretion and, like me, you should accept the situation and direct your energies toward the children. Though perhaps in your case—not wishing to criticize—I wonder if that is not at the root of your problem. You dote on those babies and seem to forget Justin has his needs, too. When were you last seen at his side?"

Cressida blinked like one dazed by blinding light. Catherine, whose lack of insight and sympathy was on a par with her lack of tactfulness, had come too close to the bone.

Seeming not to register Cressida's stricken look, her cousin went on. "I mean, have you looked at yourself lately, Cressida? Yes, at twenty-six, you still have that girlish, sleepy-eyed charm that won him over, but must you appear quite so naïve after all those children? As I said, tonight is the first time you've torn yourself from the nursery to accompany Justin anywhere, and whom do you choose to masquerade as? A shepherdess, for God's sake!" Plucking the black lace of her own daring décolletage, Catherine straightened majestically. "Justin has been your loyal husband for all these years and he loves you. But if you want to win him back from the arms of Madame Zirelli—and yes, I have it on good authority that Madame Zirelli is his new mistress—you'd do yourself more favors parading as something less"—her lip curled—"insipid."

CHAPTER 2

With Catherine thankfully departed to her own townhouse, Cressida rested her head in her hands as she slumped at her dressing table, her teeth chattering, despite the merrily blazing fire that brightened the room.

There was every chance that it was Justin who'd checked the fire was stoked and that everything was as comfortable as possible for Cressida's return. He did little things like that for her all the time.

He *loved* her!

And yet, the 'good authority' Catherine had cited was none other than Cressida's dear friend Annabelle Luscombe who'd not say a hurtful thing to a living soul.

Yes, *Annabelle* had hinted that Justin's affections had been engaged elsewhere. Not some snake-tongued society friend of Catherine's.

It was more than Cressida could bear. When she'd challenged Catherine on it, her cousin had at least had the grace to look ashamed and for a moment Cressida had believed she'd conjured up something baseless because she was jealous or because James had wounded her pride again.

Instead, Catherine had shrugged. Yes, *shrugged* and said, "Actually, the information came as quite a shock. I was in conversation with Annabelle, who was waxing lyrical over Rossini's opera *The Barber of Seville* when her husband, who is not known for his tact after three brandies, joined us, saying he'd just left Justin, who was marveling over Madame Zirelli's excellent rendering of Rosina's part. When Reggie had gone, Annabelle looked shocked, asking if Justin hadn't been known for his high regard for Madame Zirelli in the days before his marriage."

Cressida had been starting to feel marginally better. Catherine was simply making wild suppositions. Relaxing, she'd managed a smile. "And that is the only basis for these cruel rumors and gossip? The fact that Justin has been praising another woman? For her singing?" Relief had surged through her.

That is, until Catherine's viper-direct response. "Surely you must know that Madame Zirelli was Justin's mistress until five minutes before he married you?"

That's when the world had gone very quiet. And then a great roaring, whistling noise had had Cressida holding her hands to her ears.

She was holding her hands to ears once more, now, in the silence of her dressing room as memories of Catherine's false sympathy dripped like poison through her consciousness.

"Oh, my poor Cressida," her cousin had whispered before she'd quit the carriage. "How awful to be the last to know what is common knowledge. And how I wish it had not fallen to me to tell you the sordid details."

Cressida had rallied at this point. Catherine not only delivered her barbs like a skilled marksman, she savored the kill. When she'd clicked her tongue, adding in an undertone, "Let us hope the music was all he was enjoying when he paid a visit to Mrs. Plumb's notorious salon," Cressida was not going to take it like some pathetic lap dog hungry for a pat.

"That's...just cruel!" she'd managed with some energy. "Madame Plumb's is *not* the kind of establishment Justin would visit." At least on that point she could be very firm. The whispers and innu-endo that had circulated about the notorious house of assignation in Soho had penetrated even the staid and respectable circles where Cressida felt most at home. Amongst contented matrons and dowagers was where she belonged whereas Catherine belonged to a wilder set. One which Cressida had no wish to consort with.

And there was no way on earth or in heaven that Justin would step over the threshold of such a place.

Catherine, was otherwise convinced. "Indeed, I believe he has. Like Madame Zirelli, Madame Plumb, also, was an opera singer and actress before Lord Layton set her up, then after he moved on, and with Mrs. Plumb's looks too faded to snare another of his ilk, she set up her salon. It's where she's now invited Madame Zirelli to live—and to sing for her supper. Hence, Madam Plumb is now famous for her Wednesday salons. People attend in masquerade, supposedly to listen to the music, but really it's just a meeting place for—" She stopped at Cressida's gasp, saying instead, in gentler tones, "Justin has been a regular patron of Madame Plumb's, and in view of his...close relationship...with Madame Zirelli, one can only assume the reason for his visits."

"Justin loves music," Cressida had said, dully, trying to equate Justin sneaking off in masquerade to some house of ill repute after bidding her his standard, tender farewell for the evening.

The thought caused her another stab of pain, now, as she sat in the dark and tried to make sense of everything Catherine had told her.

How could Annabelle have been a party to such a sordid, demeaning conversation? Catherine had suggested Annabelle was merely distracted with having to organise the wedding of her sister-in-law's daughter. Cressida remembered again how unhappy the the bride-to-be, Miss Madeleine Hardwicke. The young woman had, in fact, looked as unhappy as Cressida felt now when Cressida had congratulated her on her impending marriage to Lord Slitherton that evening.

She tried to bolster herself with the the thought that poor Miss Hardwicke had every reason to look unhappy whereas Cressida knew that Justin still loved her—*even* if half of what Catherine had suggested was true. No, poor Miss Hardwicke was to marry someone almost old enough to be her grandfather.

Catherine hadn't been able to help herself when Cressida had turned the subject from herself to the impending nuptials. "But Lord Slitherton is rich and titled, and that's all that counts. All men—even those who are handsome or loving at the start—" she'd added, pointedly, "—stray. Oh my goodness, Cressy, you've snapped your fan!"

It had been all Cressida could do not to slap her cousin with the poor, destroyed ivory accessory Justin had given her for her last birthday. Fortunately they'd drawn to a halt in front of Catherine's townhouse just as her cousin had suggested Cressida make the most of her husband's guilt by telling her, "I suggest you order three fine, expensive gowns, confront him with everything you've heard, then present him with the bill. I promise you, he'll pay up like a lamb."

That was not how Cressida intended approaching matters though just exactly what she planned to do, she wasn't quite sure. Putting as much distance as she could between herself and her poisonous cousin had certainly been a good start, though.

THE CLOCK IN PASSAGE TOLLED ANOTHER HOUR. TWO IN THE morning. Cressida had been home for more than an hour meaning she must have been sitting here, all alone, mulling over this evening, her thoughts taking some convoluted twists and turns, for most of that time.

Hugging herself, she remembered how bolstered she'd been by her husband's praise earlier that evening.

It seemed a hundred years ago and since then the insipid shepherdess had been replaced by a lackluster creature with red-rimmed eyes and sagging shoulders.

Was Catherine right? Was Cressida really just a willfully blind and brainless wife with her head in the sand, completely unaware of her husband's desires? She shifted uncomfortably. Well, she knew about *those*. But that was now only half the problem. The other half was what he might be doing about them?

Madame Zirelli? Cressida had never even heard of her and yet this was the woman with whom her husband had had an intimate relationship right up until the moment he'd married her. That's what Catherine had said.

But what about now? Had he really returned to her?

A desolation so great she was unable to even articulate her pain washed over her. A man had needs—Cressida accepted that—and she certainly hadn't been doing what she'd *happily* done in the early years of their marriage to satisfy them.

Wearily, she justified herself, even as she knew her denial of her husband was in terms that did not reflect so much on her own fears as they might. Little Thomas was teething. He needed her. He was such a delicate child and their only son. The girls were far more robust and self-sufficient, but Thomas needed his mother. It's why Cressida slept in his nursery most nights and had done since he'd been born.

Justin knew that which was why he'd not bother to come to her bedchamber tonight. Which was just as well. Because if he did, she'd have to play the good wife and right now she didn't have it in her.

Yet she *must* speak to him.

Only...not tonight. Not so soon after what she'd learned. If she could only force herself to go to bed and get a good night's sleep, she'd wake refreshed in the morning and able to confront him as she knew she must.

And yet, a good wife turned a blind eye. She'd been taught that, too.

Her nerves were nearly at snapping point when she heard his faint footstep upon the stair even though she told herself he'd continue to his own bedchamber.

Yet how she longed to feel his arms around her.

A hardness born of fear solidified and grew within her. She knew only too well where that led.

His footsteps continued along the corridor and her heart pounded suddenly loud and insistent in her ears as she registered his pause outside her door.

Cressida squeezed shut her eyes. Justin was coming to her. She must play the good wife. She must! He loved her—and dear God, she loved him—but she was panicked. What if he—?

The door opened after a discreet knock, cutting off the thought.

"Why, Cressy, darling, what are you doing here? And all in the dark?" Justin set his candlestick upon the dressing table. "I thought you'd be with the children. Annabelle Luscombe told me you'd left the ball early. I hope you weren't feeling unwell?"

How handsome he looked, his Roman robes still crisp and immaculate after a night of revelry, concern in his voice and tenderness in his expression as he crossed the room. His lean, muscular body cast shadows across the walls. Cressida remembered how, in the past, she'd focused her attention on his flickering shadow as she'd waited with such anticipation for him to come to her. How she'd welcomed him in those early days.

Now she looked down at her lap. She'd regained her figure quickly, even after her fourth child, and was proud of the fact. But misery banished any good feeling she might have felt about the fact she'd retained her youthfulness, or even that Justin might still genuinely desire her. No, there was nothing to be proud of now when that same body that should provide for the needs of a loving husband was tense and resistant. Not when her mind silently screamed its fear that somehow Justin would unleash the gates of her latent desire and she'd succumb to—

"I'm quite well, thank you." She turned her face away as Justin lowered his head to kiss her ear, resting his hands lightly on her shoulders.

Breathing in his special scent of sandalwood, which signified safety and wonderful familiarity, she fought to remain calm.

Justin would always be the loving husband, and she would always enjoy comfort and security beyond her dreams. But now, after what Catherine had told her, despite her earlier scepticism, it seemed entirely possible that Justin had done what so many of her friends' husbands had after a certain number of years of marriage. And, if that were the case, she must find the courage to confront him then come up with the words to explain what lay behind her own withdrawal these past long months.

Instead, she sought for something...anything...to say, and burst out, "Poor Miss Hardwicke. Imagine being forced to marry someone so...old when she's in love with someone else."

Justin looked confused, as well he might since he'd just rested his cheek tenderly against his wife's. Straightening, he raised his eyebrows and, lounging against the end of Cressida's bed, asked, "Who is Miss Hardwicke?"

"Annabelle Luscombe's niece. Or rather, her sister-in-law's daughter." Cressida fiddled nervously with her silver-backed brush. "Annabelle is arranging the marriage preparations because her sister-in-law is too ill to do so."

"And, I'm afraid, that is exactly why Miss Hardwicke is marrying Lord Slitherton. Yes, of course I know now who you're referring to." He sighed. "Poor young woman will be left without a feather to fly with once her mother is gone—which is imminent, I hear, though her uncle will do what he can. He's a decent fellow. Nevertheless, it's natural Mrs Hardwicke wants to see her only child settled."

"But Miss Hardwicke is in love with Mr Pendleton!" Cressida burst out.

"Really?" Justin looked rather taken aback.

"Remember how I remarked upon how in love they looked, at a ball some months ago? You said Mr. Pendleton was marked out for great things—that is, once he's a little older and less circumspect about putting himself forward. You said he was very clever."

Justin sighed. "Sadly, Mr Pendleton's heart—and Miss Hardwicke's—is of no account when the gentleman has no money. Lord Slitherton has more than ten thousand a year."

"And so Miss Hardwicke is to spend the rest of her life in domestic slavery?"

"Domestic slavery," Justin murmured, and Cressida glanced up to see the flash of interest in his eyes.

"Oh, please don't think that's a term I've ever used in relation to my own situation," Cressida hastened to assure him, causing Justin to laugh merrily as he put his arms about her and rested his chin upon the top of her head.

The scene was one of the utmost domestic harmony, Justin's expression warm, his mood light. But that was how it always started.

Domestic felicity soon turned to tender loving which turned to...unbridled passion beneath the sheets.

Cressida's first instinct had been to raise her hand to ruffle Justin's curls, to stroke his cheek.

But memory curdled into fear and...

Cressida did what she'd done for nearly a year, since Thomas' difficult birth.

She tensed. She knew Justin registered it too, though his expression in the looking glass was as fond as ever.

Finally, she managed a smile. Not a convincing one—she could see that as much as feel it as she watched their exchange like a third person in a drama. Her hand went to the neck of her nightgown, the other fiddled with the silver-backed hairbrush she replaced, precariously, on the edge of the dressing table.

"I must say, Justin...," she stammered, lowering her eyes, "I *am* very tired."

"That makes two of us." Slowly, he began to massage her back and shoulders, and she forced herself to lean into him, nevertheless reveling in the cathartic, rhythmic strokes. If only she could be guaranteed that this was where the sensory pleasure would begin and end, then she could enjoy it.

When he began working his way down from her collarbones, his touch easing as he gently stroked the skin above the drawstring of her nightgown, there was no use even trying to pretend that she embraced, as she once had, the promise of where this may lead.

She closed her eyes and miserably went through her options, brief rage having long ago given way to despair. Though what choice was there, if indeed she had to win him back from another woman?

Could it be true, or was Catherine taunting her, playing on her insecurities?

Cressida continued to keep her eyes tightly closed so she didn't have to face the loving warmth of Justin's expression in the dim candlelight.

He wanted her and she should be drowning in joy that he still felt the same way she felt about him. She should be doing what every good wife must do. It was her duty.

But the familiar voices were screaming in her head. *Do you think, Cressida, that the rapture of a night in your husband's arms is worth the fear and pain of yet another child?*

"I must check on Thomas."

"Didn't you just do that?"

"He's suffering dreadfully with his poor little gums. He keeps waking up in great pain."

"We'd hear him, Cressy." Was that the faintest trace of exasperation she heard?

Twisting out of Justin's grip, Cressida rose, smiling as she defended herself against his increasingly rare romantic overtures, her tone the practical, sympathetic, maternal concern of a woman whose life centered on her children. Giving his arm an affectionate squeeze, she reached up to kiss him on the cheek. "He's been sleeping so fitfully, lately, that I think I'll sleep in the nursery tonight."

He did not let her go as he usually did. Halting her progress to the door, he swung her around, holding her upper arms so that, caught by surprise, she stumbled into his embrace, her head pressed against the hard muscle of his chest.

But not before she saw the hunger in his eyes. The hunger that had once thrilled and empowered her but that now filled her with dread as his gaze seemed to sear the naked flesh above the ruffled neckline of her nightgown. With a soft moan, somewhere between desire and desperation, she clung to him, but her body was, as always in such situations, rigid with terror.

For a second, she remained suspended between that and desire. If he ignored her wordless rejection, whisked her into his arms and threw her onto the bed to kiss every sensitive, exposed piece of her, it would be the first time he had put his desires before hers. She would not, could not, refuse, she knew. Her own lustful nature would take over, and she'd be a slave to passion, as in the early years of her marriage. How many times had she passed around cucumber sandwiches at her Thursday morning salon while her mind replayed the thrilling, amorous adventures to which Justin had introduced her the night before? Oh yes, during the day, she was the perfect hostess, but in the dark, beneath the sheets of the marital bed, her husband knew how to bring her to wicked rapture. The intensity of her response to him frightened her.

Sometimes she'd even wished for more, with the candle still throwing its light, so she could see what Justin looked like in all his naked splendor.

Very occasionally, at the height of passion, he'd latch on to her nipple with his hot, wet mouth, and she'd feel the pulsing desire in the core of her womb and want him to continue to pleasure her like this, here and everywhere.

But that was before the children came, and such lust was for those who spared no thought for the consequences of their pleasures.

Cressida clamped down on her moan of despair. Justin held the trump card. If she let him begin to stroke her into awareness, she knew she'd never want it to stop, and she doubted she'd have the strength to withdraw before it became dangerous. She certainly couldn't tell him about such treasonous thoughts.

Which meant she couldn't let Justin touch her any more tonight, no matter how much she desired it. Another child would kill her, yet Justin wanted another son. Young Thomas was sickly, and Cressida's most important role was to give Justin heirs. If she couldn't do that, she was no better than an insipid little shepherdess playing dress up. She could respond with soft murmurs indicating her delight in bed, but right now she did not have the words to tell him she'd not give him more sons. She wondered if she ever would.

Cressida seized the advantage at his hesitation. Justin was not a man to press his unwanted advances upon her. Clasping him briefly before pushing out of his arms, she made for the door where, turning, she was surprised to see how much her brief, affectionate embrace had disarmed him.

He remained in the center of her dressing room, fiddling with his cufflinks, his concentration seemingly focused on the tiny diamond studs at his wrists. When he straightened and smiled at her, her armor was not fully in place against the hurt in his eyes. It pierced her with a sharpness and intensity nearly as agonizing as childbirth, forcing her to turn away before she acted against her better judgment.

Self-disgust surged up her gullet as she turned the doorknob. So much for acting on her desperation to reclaim what they'd once had; for taking the bold step needed following Catherine's revelation. Her shame that she was pushing him away from her was almost equal to her shame at realizing that her actions confirmed she had chosen to accept the price.

With no satisfaction in the marital bed, what other course was there for a red-blooded male?

"Sleep well, Cressida." There was such genuine fondness in his expression as he prepared to leave her that she nearly abandoned her resolve by throwing herself recklessly into his arms.

"You too, Justin."

He was nearly gone when she stopped him. Her throat was dry, but she had to know his plans for the rest of this evening, though couched in such a way that no invitation could be forthcoming if perchance he was going straight to bed.

"Will you join me for breakfast?" she asked, smiling her false, bright smile.

"If you wish it." By contrast, he was no longer smiling. "However, I feel restless. I know I shan't sleep." Indeed, he did look distracted—and little wonder—his gaze fixed on a point somewhere near the window. "I think perhaps I'll return to White's. Roddy Johnson was still there when I left and had, I think, plans for a night on the town."

Only when she was safely in the nursery and satisfied that little Thomas was sleeping peacefully did Cressida return to her chamber and give vent to her feelings. Sinking back down upon the stool in front of her dressing table, she rested her head upon her arms and sobbed.

CHAPTER 3

T he revelry into which he'd thrown himself at White's after he'd left Cressida the previous night hadn't been the antidote for which Justin had hoped.

He'd slept late, which was unusual for him. When he'd appeared in the breakfast parlor and been told his wife had gone out, Justin was ashamed of the relief that had washed over him as he'd dished up his eggs and haddock from the sideboard.

The truth was, he didn't know how to look her in the eye after their awkward pre-dawn parting.

Now, a wearying day had passed during which Justin had attended to certain pressing matters on behalf of a friend. Fortunately the surprising request had managed to divert him for most of the day during which he'd been too busy to dwell on his lack of courage when it came to discussing, in clear and direct terms, the nature of the impasse that clearly had developed between him and his wife.

Five o' clock came and went. Cressida was still out shopping. Or she was visiting Catherine who'd entertained her to luncheon or some such thing. Justin couldn't quite recall the reason she wasn't at home when it came time for him to leave and discharge a potentially awkward duty he couldn't begin to explain to Cressida.

He was just glad he wasn't going to be called upon to answer any questions she might have as to where he intended to spend most of the coming evening.

Dressing carefully, he left the house on foot, then signalled for a hackney to take him the rest of the way.

It was a grey, dull evening with more than a hint of chill in the air which matched Justin's mood. Increasingly, he found it hard to summon up the lightness of spirit that had characterised the early years of his marriage.

And yet, marriage to Cressida had given him more happiness than he could quantify. Even if her ardor had waned, he still wanted her.

It was the thought that her affections might have strayed that bothered him more than anything else.

"Stop!" He rapped on the roof with his cane, jumped out into the cobbled street, then paid the jarvey before treading with dull resignation up to the railing, hesitating at the base of the three stone steps that led to the front door.

Glancing up, he saw a face at the window of one of the upstairs rooms. To all appearances, the house seemed respectable enough. The comings and goings might arouse suspicion, but both gentlemen *and* ladies from society's highest echelons regularly stepped over the threshold, albeit usually disguised in some manner.

On this occasion, Justin had not resorted to more than a simple masque, though he was regretting that as he stepped aside to allow a large woman wearing an elaborate, ostrich-plumed face mask that hid most of her features to pass him on the steps. She was leaning heavily on the arm of a small, slender gentleman, clearly years younger than herself, and a glance at the richness of her gown, which even Justin could tell was embellished with this season's trimmings, suggested she was not some tawdry imposter of the aristocracy. Justin recoiled in sudden shock when he heard her throaty murmur. Good Lord, could this really be Lady Dalton? He turned his face away, fearing she'd recognize him. This was not a place either of them would wish to be known to frequent.

The door opened then, and Lady Dalton—if that's who she was—and her mismatched companion lurched past him and down the corridor as if they knew exactly where they were headed.

Justin, by contrast, handed his hat and cane to a young girl barely older than his daughter, he reflected uncomfortably, who led him into Mrs. Plumb's oddly decorated, little sitting room, for the handsome paintings and sculptures contrasted strangely with the knick-knacks that might have been collected by a simple cottager's daughter—though rumor had it that's what Mrs. Plumb had been when she'd arrived in the city to work as a housemaid before catching the eye of a wealthy banker, the first of a number of liaisons that had secured her future.

He should not be here, he thought again as he was led to a cluster of chairs. Though this might not be a brothel in the finer sense of the word, it was little better—although there were those who claimed to come only for the music and to cure their loneliness through conversation. Madame Plumb's previous premises near the Haymarket had been a much wilder place but as she'd got older she'd catered to a more sober clientele.

It was, he supposed, why Madame Zirelli was able to make a home here.

A howl of raucous laughter erupted from somewhere above him and was followed by a moan of apparent ecstasy from a room nearby. Justin felt increasingly uncomfortable. The contrast with his own domestic haven could not have been more stark. Men and women came here to seek pleasure when pleasure was lacking in their own homes, their own lives.

But Justin was not one of those. He had a beautiful, loving wife waiting for him. A wife who, if anything, was more exquisite than the day he met her. Even after four children and eight years of marriage, he still desired Cressida more than he had desired any woman. Ever.

Fidgeting while he waited, he glanced up at a painting on the wall depicting a couple in a the throes of unbridled passion. The woman was pale and beautifully rounded with pert breasts, long golden tresses, wearing nothing more than an expression of the greatest rapture as she writhed in the arms of a handsome adonis.

An uncensored image of Cressida's pale limbs, fully exposed in the dawn light flashed through his mind, making him squirm. A long time had passed since he'd woken beside her after a night of passion, conducted as was usual, in the dark. He remembered one occasion, as he'd rolled over sleepily to pull her against his chest, he'd been jolted by the sight of the sun slanting through a chink in the curtain, burnishing the naked limbs of his sleeping wife. Even now the memory made his throat dry for he'd rarely seen her fully exposed.

How innocent she'd looked, her lips curved in a slight smile, her hair loosened and spread about her like a halo. He had gazed at her for what seemed like hours, drinking in every curve of her body, which he knew like a treasure map by touch but which, he now reflected sadly, he'd never seen by daylight and, rarely, by candlelight. He'd been riveted, in fact. How elegantly her limbs melded from dainty feet and ankles to finely tuned calves, thighs, then to that secret juncture, thatched with fine blond hair.

Justin had no idea how long he'd had gazed at her, drinking in the beauty of her body. She'd woken when he'd touched her, his hand lightly skimming her curves, cupping her pubic mound. In the dark, during their frequent lovemaking, she'd indicated her pleasure at being touched there, but in the daylight, shock and embarrassment scarred her expression and she'd scrambled to pull down the thin linen night rail always present between them, even in the midst of the most passionate of lovemaking. But she had been an enthusiastic participant. Her murmurs and responses had indicated that, hadn't they?

Fearfully, he tried to remember the last encounter where she'd exhibited signs of pleasure.

In fact, the last time they had made love.

He ran his forefinger around his collar that suddenly seemed too tight and wished he was wearing last night's fancy dress. Not only was a toga more comfortable to wear, it made it easier to pretend that everything was still perfect between himself and Cressida when, clearly, it was not.

Memory returned. Yes, the last time they'd made love was several months after Millie's birth, and in fact, a few hours before Dr. Milner had examined Cressida and announced she was with child again. Their third. Naturally, Cressida had been over the moon, though Justin remembered his twinge of disappointment at the knowledge that he would have to resist his wife and keep his hands off her during her later months of breeding. For that was how it was, and not to be questioned.

With each successive child, the passion between them was diluted as Cressida focused more on the infants than on him, as he supposed was to be expected. Some men would have sought pleasure elsewhere, still loyal to their roles as husbands and fathers but comfortably justifying their need for sexual diversion.

Not Justin. He wanted no other woman, and besides, it would destroy Cressida if she ever learned of such a betrayal.

So when the young servant girl entered the room, simpering as she asked with clear innuendo if there was anything else he required for his comfort, Justin shook his head, conscious more than ever of the smell of cheap perfume that wafted through from the other rooms of the house while suffering more than a twinge of guilt at being here. Cressida's sensibilities would be highly offended by even the existence of such an establishment. If she ever learned he'd stepped over the threshold she was quite likely to jump to the worst conclusion.

The young girl disappeared into the shadows after announcing Madame Zirelli and Justin removed his masquerade mask as the door opened.

He rose as she entered, noticing the heaviness of her movements when she'd once been all light and energy. It sharpened the
edge of his guilt—both for the fact he wished he were not here,
and for feeling that way.

"It was good of you to come again, Justin." His old friend's
smile was tired, again with no trace of the radiance he remembered from days gone by. Even in the few weeks since he'd acceded
to her extraordinary summons so many years after they'd last
parted, she seemed to have faded.

"Mariah." He clasped her hand in both of his, conscious as he'd
never been before of the great weight of sadness she carried. And
of what she'd once been to him. Mariah had altered greatly in the
years since he'd first met her, but she was still a beauty. Now,
though, she looked as if she carried the weight of the world on her
shoulders.

Mariah smiled wearily. "My boy got your message a short while
ago. I appreciate you making the time to see me when I know how
busy you must be. I was afraid that family considerations might
prevent you from coming to see me."

There was no trace of bitterness in her wry smile. In her
maturer years, she was still striking for her regal grace transcended
aging. Only a few strands of gray peppered her almost blue-black
hair, and her body was as fine as he remembered it. But her heart
had been broken, and the melancholy that had leeched her
vibrancy tugged at his heartstrings. Mariah had been dealt a
cruel hand.

"You know I could never refuse you, Mariah," he said,
accepting a glass of brandy from the young servant who discreetly
left them alone after plumping a few cushions and tending to the
small fire.

She gave a little laugh and reached over to pat his thigh. "I
think you could," she said, "if I were to overreach myself. Everyone
tells me what a loyal and devoted husband and father you are
these days."

Impulsively, he reached over and took her hand, surprising

himself. She gripped it, and for a moment, he was afraid she wasn't about to let it go. But she was too shrewd not to understand the delicate boundaries of their altered relationship, and she gave it an almost maternal pat before releasing it.

"Devoted, my dear Mariah," he corroborated in a murmur, his mind replaying the painful events of his parting the previous night with his beloved and increasingly distant wife.

Yet whatever happened, he'd always be devoted to Cressida. His visit here had been prompted as much by a need to unburden himself as to respond to Mariah's summons but it suddenly seemed a betrayal of his intimacy with Cressida to hint at domestic discord.

Yet surely the advice of a sensible woman would not go astray? There were few of those in his life, he reflected, thinking of his mother, who now lived with them, and of Cressida's frightful cousin, Catherine. Perhaps Mariah, as a kind woman with considerable experience of life, could offer some insight into the reasons for Cressida's withdrawal the past ten months.

He drained his brandy and set down his glass. First, though, it was understandable that Mariah would be anxious to learn the progress he'd made concerning her unexpected request several weeks ago. A request he was possibly in a position to discharge though he feared the answers promised only heartache. There was much to admire in this woman who had suffered with such dignity and Justin had no wish to add to her pain.

Sensing his uncertainty, she became businesslike. "You have discovered something, Justin, and I have not the patience to wait for you to tell me in your own words and time. I am sure you wish to be on your way, too."

Justin nodded. "You *have* waited a long time, Mariah. I understand that." He weighed up the kindest way to couch his response when he had no news to gladden her heart. Directness was always the best way forward, he decided, before reflecting he and Cressida had been anything but direct with one another lately. "There are several possibilities, Mariah."

"*Several?*" She took a breath, drawing herself up and fixing him with an incisive look.

One dainty, black slipper peeped from beneath the flounce of her once fashionable cerulean gown. Mariah had always dressed elegantly, but in the dim light, Justin could see the signs of wear, the discreet darning.

"Yet nothing conclusive?"

He shook his head. For a long time there was silence. "Mariah, if you need money—"

She raised her hand, cutting him off. "I sing for my supper every Wednesday, Justin. Mrs. Plumb has been a good friend." She indicated the small drawing room in which they sat. "She gives me my privacy when I need it and ensures I do not lack entertainment."

Justin gave a wry laugh and patted his masque beside him. "I wish it weren't necessary to disguise myself, Mariah. I feel like a thief in the night and don't know how I'd begin to explain these visits to my wife."

"Your wife should value even more the prize jewel she married. You've not told her about what you're doing, Justin? You promised me you would."

His urge to confide in Mariah about his marital problems was checked by her mild criticism of Cressida, and he regretted unburdening himself when he'd hinted that his wife was no longer as eager for the joys of the marital bed as she once had been. But it had been so good to see Mariah again after so many years and natural to revive the friendship with its old familiarity.

"Cressida is an angel. I'd trust her with my life, but since you are concerned that she mixes with some of the parties involved in my investigation, I assure you that my lips are sealed."

"Cressida is a lucky woman."

Justin glanced at Mariah's face, serene and faintly sympathetic in the light cast by the Argand light on the low table nearby. He did not think jealousy was behind the faint contempt he sensed. Mariah and he had shared similar interests and an affectionate rather than passionate physical relationship all those years ago. He'd been generous when he'd given Mariah her *congé,* though her illustrious marriage to Lord Grainger ought to have ensured her comfort for the rest of the days.

It was, in fact, when Mariah looked set to be left all but destitute by the aging peer who was in the process of divorcing her that she and Justin had met. Mariah had already risen to great heights in her own right when she'd won Grainger's heart. The once-famous opera singer had gone on to win Justin's after she'd sought legal advice while struggling to maintain her dignity—and enough support to keep body and soul together—in the face of Grainger's appalling treatment of her during the final months of their marriage. Mariah had given the youthful Justin her loyalty and her gratitude for his friendship. Much later, she'd given him her body. What she hadn't given him were satisfying reasons for her humiliating divorce. Faithless on her part had not been one of them, anyway.

"It seems Cressida would rather put you through the mill than offer a reasonable argument for her cruelty. You don't suspect she has a lover?"

Two days ago, the suggestion would have been implausible. Nevertheless, Justin forced a laugh. "You always were my champion, my dear Mariah," he said, "but since you have never met my wife, I beg you to refrain from passing judgment. I must be blamed for this erroneous perception of her, for, I assure you, a man could have no better wife." Smiling, refusing to countenance the churning in his breast, he added, "Cressida is the most conscientious of mothers. It is a trial and a sadness that our youngest is not robust, but I will not hear Cressida criticized for choosing her son's comfort over mine on occasion."

"Perceptions matter as much as the truth." Mariah fixed him with a direct look. "The word about town is that Lady Lovett has not been seen more than three times by your side during the last year. You are lonely, Justin."

The concern in her expression was genuine, not a gambit for offering him the solace of her charms.

Indeed, it was on account of his genuine liking and respect for his old friend and former mistress that Justin allowed her to persist with the subject.

"Have you *never* suspected there might be someone else, Justin?"

When he shook his head, she countered, gently, "I was married to Lord Grainger for many years. I thought I knew him better than I knew myself. It was only in the final year of our marriage that I discovered I did not know him at all."

This was not the time to question Mariah about her husband or to put his own marriage to such close, uncomfortable scrutiny. Justin rose and went to the window. "As I have already made plain, Mariah, nothing stands between Cressida and me except"— holding back the curtain, he stared into the moonless night—"the children." It was the first time he'd put it into words. A vision of their young, happy faces blurred in his mind. Unhappily, he added, "They are everything to her."

"Children play an essential part in the success of a marriage, as I well know"—her voice wavered—"but they cannot provide her with *everything* she needs, Justin."

He glanced over his shoulder. "I'm sorry, Mariah, it was thoughtless of me—"

"You are too sensitive if you thought your words implied that, just as your many children may be the reason for your troubles, the lack of children was the *entire* reason for my divorce and current situation."

He no longer wanted to pursue this line. Mariah was quite likely to prise from him deeper pain and grievances than he wished to articulate.

"Cressida has given me three healthy daughters and a son, yet I am as drawn by her beguiling charm as I was the day we met." He realized the words sounded trite and rehearsed. Forcing himself to cast aside his despondency, he began to pace. "She is an extraordinary woman and, just as she is devoted to family life, I am devoted to her."

Mariah gave a desultory little clap. "Bravo, Justin. I wish all husbands were as loyal to their wives as you are to your Cressida. I hope she may yet prove she deserves you."

From the window embrasure, Justin turned. "She does so every day. Cressida is kind and gentle, and it is only natural that with the arrival of so many in the nursery, she is less driven by the carnal desires which curse we men." With a restless sigh, he returned to the sofa, giving Mariah a rueful smile. "You sought my services in the hope I might put an end to your pain and suffering by at least supplying you with an answer to the one question that has haunted you for eighteen years—the identity and location of your daughter." Taking her hand, he squeezed it lightly. "Though so different from my wife, you are a woman, Mariah, who craves the same things Cressida does, the joy of seeing one's children grow. Ironically, Cressida has this in such abundance she no longer needs me as much as she once did. I have her love and affection, and I tell myself it should be enough." He shrugged, as if it didn't hurt. "I'm following your investigation for you as a friend and, as discussed, I refuse payment for these services. But..." He dissembled, unsure where his thoughts were taking him. Deciding there was no need to censor the activity of his brain, he proceeded with unusual recklessness, his throat suddenly dry as he realized how much he wanted advice. "But, Mariah, as a friend, and a woman experienced in life's sorrows and disappointments, perhaps I could ask from you some small payment? Perhaps you could tell me plainly if you believe all hope is lost." He hesitated. "And, if not, suggest how I might rekindle my wife's desire?"

Mariah's look was kind. In the manner of her countrywomen, she gave an expressive shrug. "Have you tried talking to her? That's always a good beginning."

"I hear the irony in your tone, and I concede that words are the obvious, but sometimes the hardest, way to begin." Frustrated, he added, "Cressida knew *nothing* about relations between men and women when I married her, though she seemed to have no aversion to her...bedroom duties." Indeed, her unexpected enthusiasm and the heights of passion that had quickly elevated their relationship beyond the early kindling of their love could not have been feigned.

Until Thomas' birth. No... She had withdrawn long before that. Not just in the purely physical sense, in the bedroom. Once, they'd kissed and cuddled but it had been a long time since they'd done even that.

With three children in the nursery, her wifely devotions had swung definitely in favor of motherly duties, though it was only in the past ten months she had developed the regular megrims that seemed to coincide with any visit he made to her bedchamber.

"Cressida was obviously born to be a mother." He raked his hand through his hair. The evening had been most unsatisfactory. He could tell Mariah nothing that would give her comfort with regard to her search for her lost child, meanwhile, Mariah's mild criticism of Cressida needled him, though he'd pressed on to discuss the marital problems that neither he nor his wife seemed able to broach.

He picked up his demi-mask as he prepared to leave, returning to the subject of the business that had first brought them together. Briskly, he said, "I have been stringing out your anticipation by talking of my marital concerns when I intended merely to tell you that I have found not one, but two, likely avenues to pursue. Next time I visit, I shall have the list of the children who were admitted to and removed from the Sedleywich Home for Orphans in the years in which you are interested, Mariah. My report is begun, and I am following your lead, though I must tell you now, if your suspicion is correct, great effort has gone into muddying the trail that might reveal your daughter's new identity. I should know before the end of the week."

Mariah clasped her hands to her heart. "You are a good man, Justin, and you have always been kind to me. Thank you for coming here tonight when, really, you have little to impart to give me hope. And yet, I do still hope."

Her smile was tinged with the radiance he remembered. "If I can do anything in return, it would be to suggest that when you get home, take your wife into your arms, and ask her what is troubling her. Words may be the hardest way to broach the subject, but you have to give her the opportunity to say what's in her heart before you reveal the state of yours."

CHAPTER 4

"**Y**ou have a visitor, ma'am."

Cressida's heart sank. Millie, the parlormaid always adopted that tone when it was Catherine. Disdainful and under sufferance. It was just the way Cressida felt only she was too well bred to show it.

"Please, show her in."

A visit from her cousin was the last thing she desired but Catherine was never one to wait. Even if Cressida had instructed the parlor maid to say that her mistress was out, Catherine would have barged in before Cressida had a chance to escape.

And then there'd have been hell to pay.

So, as Catherine breezed into the drawing room and settled her lanky, horsey frame onto the green plush sofa, remarking, "You don't look at all yourself, Cressy, darling. Surely you're still not mulling over what we spoke about the other night," Cressida had to dig her fingernails into her palms to restrain any possibly unwise remark.

Four long days ago. The longest of her life.

"Of course not." She hoped she sounded chilly enough to deflect the subject or that she could come up with inspiration for something to divert Catherine who was always like a dog with a bone when she discovered a person's raw nerve.

"Well, I sincerely hope you're not," Catherine said, almost brightly as she pulled the bell rope to order tea for them both. She'd always behaved as if she owned the place. "You forget how lucky you were, Cressy, that you were able to follow your heart, marry money and that you retained your husband's interest for so long. Just because Justin has taken a mistress doesn't mean you are less to him than you ever were. He just wants more. Like most men."

Cressida glared at her cousin and darted a quick glance about her to make sure none of the servants was in earshot. "I don't for one minute believe he's taken a mistress, Catherine. But since you've clearly decided he's consorting with this Madame Zirelli, perhaps you'd like to tell me a bit about her. I've never heard of her."

She was encouraged by the skepticism with which she managed to lace lace her tone, disappointed when Catherine responded matter-of-factly, "Neither had I, until Annabelle told me the curious story of Miss Hardwicke's uncle's determination that Madame Zirelli sing at his niece's wedding."

"Miss Hardwicke's uncle? Sir Robert, do you mean?" Cressida frowned. She'd heard Annabelle mention this illustrious member of the family who'd made a great fortune across the seas and had never been back to England.

"That's right. Well, he's coming back for Miss Hardwicke's wedding, and of course Annabelle is doing all the organizing as Miss Hardwicke's poor mother is on her deathbed—"

"But what's Sir Robert got to do with Madame Zirelli?" *What did this have to do with Justin?* Cressida leaned forward to quiz her. Catherine was wrong.

"Well, Sir Robert has lived abroad the past sixteen years, in case you didn't know, and he's returning for the wedding but with the oddest request. He charged Annabelle with the task of hunting down the finest soprano in all England and has especially instructed Annabelle to seek out this Madame Zirelli." Catherine leaned back and her voice took on an edge of scorn. "Of course, Annabelle's husband took over the search after Annabelle learned of Madame Zirelli's...well, unsavory past...and it led him to Mrs. Plumb's house of ill repute."

"Then naturally Justin is merely helping to locate this Madame Zirelli." *That was it! What a joyful discovery!*

Catherine raised an eyebrow. "And it would seem Justin knew just where to look." She sighed as if her cousin were displaying the greatest ignorance.

"Surely, Cressida, you can't imagine your husband led a blameless life before he whisked you down the aisle? Be glad his name is associated with only this one woman. Why, James—"

But Cressida wasn't interested in James. James was a whoremonger. Innocent though she was, she'd heard the label used in association with her cousin's husband, and for that reason alone, she must try and feel some sympathy for Catherine, who'd never known the love and loyalty Cressida had taken for granted all these years.

At last Cressida had discovered the logic behind the terrible innuendo and she'd never felt stronger. "I'm sorry, Catherine, but I don't take everything at face value like you do. Justin is deeply loyal. I have never found fault with him as either a husband or a father." Her thoughts trailed away. It was true, though, that she knew nothing of Justin's female associations before she'd married him.

But then a terrible thought occurred and without stopping to think, she blurted out, "This Madame Zirelli...if indeed Justin did have an association with her... Perhaps she was not someone he could marry—" The idea of Justin losing his heart to someone else before her time but being unable to follow his inclinations was a terrible one and put their entire marriage in a new light.

"Without wishing to sound unkind, you were hardly a glittering prospect, Cressy." With some slight consideration for the bluntness of this assessment, Catherine hurried on at her cousin's injured look, reminding her of what Cressida had always taken comfort in. "Justin lost his heart to you the moment he saw you, and, despite all the persuasion that could be exerted, he married you, penniless though you were. This Madame Zirelli was married to Lord Grainger, though I believe their divorce was being finalized when she and Justin— Well, anyway, suffice to say you must forget this foolish idea that Justin is returning to some long-lost love."

Cressida closed her eyes briefly, opening them on a smile as Mille returned bearing the tea tray.

"I'll pour," she murmured, leaning over to perform the niceties while her mind whirled over a million possibilities.

"You'll pour." Catherine gave a world-weary sigh. "Is that all you can say? Is that all you can do?"

Helplessly, with the tea pot in mid air, Cressida stared at her cousin. "What else *can* I do?"

"You can tackle Justin on the matter or you can investigate. The latter is what I'd do."

"But I'm not you and we're so—"

Catherine was staring at her with raised eyebrows. "Different?" she supplied. "Yes, I'm the brazen siren and you're the insipid shepherdess yet do we not both seek the same thing? Satisfaction?"

"Happiness is the word I've have used," Cressida murmured, casting her cousin her most demure look while inside she raged.

"So, what are you going to do?"

"I will speak to Justin," Cressida muttered, putting down the teapot with a clatter.

"*Speak* to him? Why, if these are nothing but rumors, as you're so sure is the case, you'll not want to wound darling Justin's sensibilities by suggesting you believe ill of him."

"Well, I can hardly don a disguise and start creeping after him at all hours of the night!" Cressida snapped.

Catherine shrugged, her eyes glittering over the rim of the teacup she raised to her lips. "And why not? You must discover the truth for yourself and make the most of the power you have over him, Cressy. We women have little enough of it."

❧

SHE MIGHT RESENT CATHERINE; SHE MIGHT THINK HER BRAZEN and insufferable. A bully.

But Cressida could see the merit of her cousin's outrageous, terrifying words. If she couldn't simply return to offering her husband the full conjugal rights he was entitled to as per their marriage contract, and if she couldn't find the courage to explain her fears, and question him directly, then she must find some other means of learning, exactly, Justin was doing. Only then could she decide how far she could tolerate the current situation.

Madam Plumb's Salon.

Catherine had the address at her fingertips and now Cressida had no excuse, for once again Justin had chosen to spend the evening away from her.

There was a distinct chill in the night air as she stepped out of her hired hackney and her hands felt cold and clammy in their York tan gloves as she fought for the courage to raise the polished brass door knocker of the unassuming, four square house in front of her. Everything seemed so alien, so frightening, without her husband or the children, or even a maid, beside her.

But Cressida was *not* going to become an object of gossip or remain a miserable wife without first trying to discover the truth for herself. Several times during the past couple of days she'd caught Justin staring at her. Once, locking glances, he'd opened his mouth as if he would say something, his look meaningful. But a maid had entered the breakfast room and the conversation had then turned to the food—followed, as usual, by the children.

Then, yesterday, after the pudding had been cleared away and Cressida and Justin were alone for a few moments in the dining room, battling, it seemed, with an oppressive silence, Cressida had been the one to initiate an exchange.

But she'd got no further then, "Justin, I—" before words failed her.

She closed her eyes and shuddered at the horror of ending that sentence. *Justin, I want to know if you have a mistress.* If she couldn't even think it, then how could she say it to Justin? No, it couldn't be true. And she did not have the fortitude for how disappointed Justin would be in her if he knew she seriously doubted his constancy when it wasn't true.

That was what she'd come to verify tonight—and didn't it make her feel a thief in the night? Justin's love, she knew she had in abundance, but his constancy...? If he had strayed, she had only herself to blame.

With the door knocker still in her hand, she reflected on a boldness she'd not dreamed she possessed. All those things Catherine had accused her of returned like a shower of reproach. First she'd exhorted Cressida to learn the truth for herself. Then her cousin had become sneering and disdainful as she'd gone on to advise Cressida to accept the inevitable as Catherine had done years ago. It was true that Cressida was timid by nature, and certainly compared with Cousin Catherine, but she could not allow Catherine to brand Justin complacently as no better than any other man.

The ring of the horses' hooves as the hackney that had dropped her here now disappeared around the corner was the loneliest, most frightening noise she had ever heard. In her whole life, she'd never been alone or unaccompanied after dark. Nannies, governesses, Justin and then children had accompanied her everywhere.

Adjusting the thick gauze veil over her face, Cressida took three deep breaths for courage and knocked loudly. She was trembling so much she thought she'd crumple upon the spot.

She took a shaky breath. She had to follow through with this. Succumbing to her usual fear was not an option. She had to be able to inform Catherine that her husband had never set foot within the notorious—as she'd now learned Mrs. Plumb's salon definitely was—den of vice and iniquity. Regardless of what she discovered, she'd tell Catherine that, anyway. No, Cressida had to know for *herself*.

Within seconds of her knock, she was admitted into a dim, quiet passage lined with paintings of women in various states of undress, the heavy atmosphere overlaid by a strong scent of musk. She felt the thickness of her veil for reassurance as she battled to combat the nausea caused by the sudden surge of fear before pressing her hands briefly against the passage wall to steady herself.

She could do this. She had to do this.

Her courage was bolstered by the sound of a confident contralto issuing through the door that had been opened for her by a slip of a parlor maid. Italian opera... Excitement mingled with trepidation as the girl took her cloak and the distant sound of clapping carried through from the next room.

However, by the time Cressida had settled herself on a blue brocade chair, she was dismayed to find a tall, balding young man offering the company—of about thirty, altogether—a passionate recitation of a passage from *Ivanhoe*. If only Cressida had timed her arrival a few minutes earlier, but Thomas had been fractious, and— She stopped mid-thought. The truth was that, although Justin was out, she had searched for just about every excuse not to come this evening and face her terrors.

Now her usual prevarication, if not cowardice, had resulted in the loss of her prime opportunity for seeing for herself this Madame Zirelli—whom Catherine claimed had ensnared her husband, a theory Cressida was desperate to discount— before deciding how best to act.

Casting around the room for a woman who fitted the vague description Catherine had given her of a dark-haired woman nearing forty, she decided Madame Zirelli had quit the scene of her rousing performance.

Of course, no one with pretensions to respectability would be seen dead at Madam Plumb's, which was why most of those assembled were in masquerade while another handful were, like herself, heavily veiled.

Smoothing the skirts of her black silk gown, Cressida tried to swallow down her nervousness at seeing several gentlemen whom she knew were acquaintances of Justin. Of Justin, however, there was no sign, which made her vague, desperate plan seem all the more ill-conceived and not properly thought out. Was it any wonder her husband had grown tired of a wife who seemed capable of little more than nursing his children?

Clapping dutifully as the current performer, the dome-headed orator, came to the end of his repertoire, her mind focused on her next move. What if someone addressed her? Asked her name? She had no idea how matters were conducted in a place like this, or indeed what went on other than music and conversation, though she could not plead complete ignorance. Catherine had taken such delight in telling Cressida about what kind of salon Mrs. Plumb ran. Cressida knew most wives would believe they had no choice but to turn a blind eye. They certainly wouldn't venture out to visit such a salon as Cressida was doing right now. Perhaps most wives would consider Mrs. Plumb was doing a service, providing a meeting place for nefarious assignations in the dim chambers beyond if their husbands considered their amatory needs were not being met by their wives. Perhaps most wives considered that such discretion shown by their husbands, in avoiding bawdy houses or more public *carte blanches*, was acceptable. The idea sickened Cressida. It made her feel physically ill to think of what Catherine had said. That people like Justin—and even apparently well-connected, irreproachable women like herself—came here to meet a lover. If Catherine were with her, her cousin would no doubt claim that Justin and the Italian warbler she had heard on her arrival were closeted together at this moment, engaged in the very activities Cressida had once enjoyed so greatly but that now terrified her.

Covering her face with her hands, she recalled Catherine's gleeful revelations. She must not dwell on them. After all, it was only gossip, and Catherine thrived on gossip. It was to settle her doubts that she had come here.

Even as she tried to bolster herself with this, she acknowledged that as Justin was rarely home these days, she must assume he was seeking company more diverting than her own.

She was only half aware of the emptying of the drawing room—the withdrawal of patrons into chambers beyond while those remaining made small talk around a table of glazed ham and plover's eggs.

Her misery enveloped her like a cloak of heavy, green slime. Could it be true? Could Justin be amongst those who'd silently slid into the shadows? Oh, she was certain she retained her husband's heart and his regard, but what was a man to do when denied his physical needs? Cressida had barely let him do more than caress her in ten months.

"Would you care for some refreshment, madam?"

It was Mrs. Plumb, judging by the description Catherine had given her. Coarse, plump Mrs. Plumb, dressed like Cressida in respectable widow's weeds, smiling unctuously at her as she offered her a fizzing champagne coupe. Glancing about her, Cressida realized she was alone amidst a sea of empty blue brocade chairs.

The woman leaned closer, and her smile was conspiratorial. "Or perhaps there is a certain gentleman, known or otherwise, to whom you seek an introduction. Madame Plumb prides herself on ensuring the pleasure of her patrons." She thrust out her hand and gripped Cressida's wrist. "Madam, are you all right?"

The woman's vulgar words brought the bile rushing up Cressida's throat. Pushing away, she hurried toward the door, past a knot of people gathered near the supper table, to find herself in a darkened passage. What on earth had possessed her to come to such a place? She was out of her mind. Without doubt, she was out of her depth.

In the gloom, she observed a gentleman walking down the corridor, head bent, but when he raised it, as he drew almost level, he was smiling at her. And there was invitation implicit in the sweep of his speculative gaze.

Fear and horror propelled Cressida through the first door she came to, hoping wildly it would offer an escape route to the street outside. She had to get as far away as she could from Mrs. Plumb, her patrons and their odious assumptions. Who knew what the woman was going to suggest for Cressida's entertainment? A quick fumble with that man who looked like he was treading the corridors in search of conquest? He'd been handsome enough, but not so young that there wasn't someone at home waiting for him?

Madam Plumb's establishment was not a place for a gently reared female, and the sooner Cressida was back home where she belonged, the better. It was time to admit defeat. With relief, she decided that this was definitely a place Justin would *never* visit.

Closing the door behind her, she closed her eyes as she sank against it, waiting for the drumming in her mind to abate. Blessed relief it was to be alone, though she wouldn't rest until she'd found her way onto the street and freedom. Her hand were clammy with fear and her mouth was dry, but a calming scent of rosewater dissipated her nausea. After a moment, she became conscious of a faint singing in the background—soft, gentle, harmonious voices.

Disoriented, Cressida opened her eyes and gazed upon the countenance of the most angelic creature she'd ever seen.

"Have you come to join us?" asked the young woman, who smiled when Cressida jerked back in fear.

Dressed in flowing, diaphanous robes, her long, fair hair rippled from a high Madonna forehead, and her eyes were blue and guileless. "My name is Ariane." There was something mesmerizing about her gaze and, as if she had no will of her own, Cressida stretched out her hands as Ariane whispered, "You look as if you have lost your way and don't know how to find it again." She squeezed Cressida's hand unleashing a powerful sense of comfort and hope. "I think I understand, for I was once like you—fearful. But there's nothing to be afraid of in this house. Not if you are looking for love."

Oh, she was looking for love but not the kind that could be found in a house like this.

Strangely, though, the young woman's gaze was compelling enough to keep Cressida rooted to the spot. What could be the harm if she stayed a little? There were only women in this room, after all, for she could see several in the background through the strange mist-like substance that seemed to have been part of their performance.

Cressida glanced from her severe garments of disguise to the young woman before her. Everyone tonight had been dressed in masquerade but this young woman looked as if she had nothing to hide, as if she'd stepped straight from a mythical painting, adding to Cressida's sense of unreality that she should be in such a place. Ariane was the most beautiful woman Cressida had ever laid eyes upon. She was also the most undressed, with her gossamer robes leaving little to the imagination.

Blushing, Cressida realised their hands were now linked, while this young woman, Ariane, was one of four similarly dressed 'goddesses' in the room. All smiled kindly at her with understanding in their eyes. Suddenly, she felt emboldened.

"I don't know why I came," she blurted out. "I heard men and women meet lovers in this house. But that's not why I came. I haven't come to meet a lover." Fearful, suddenly, of being misconstrued, she pulled away her hands and backed toward the door. "I'm not like that." She tried to steady her breathing. "I saw a man in the corridor just now who looked at me as if I were like—"

"Like one of us?" Ariane supplied with a smile. She'd followed and now began to stroke Cressida's arm, her soft, ungloved touch searing sensation through her. "A Vestal Virgin? That's what we're called, you know." Ariane's laugh was a more sensual than Cressida would have expected. "If he was dark and handsome with a piratical leer, then he was probably my husband."

"Your husband?"

Ariane nodded. "You sound shocked. Yet Mrs. Plumb's Salon of Sin is for everyone like us—star-crossed lovers or those burdened by unhappy marriages." She began to stroke Cressida's forearm as she led her around the room. "My husband and I eloped five years ago, but it's a secret we must keep until he turns five-and-twenty and can therefore claim his inheritance." She sighed. "So we meet here, where I survive by dancing for the entertainment of others. We all have a different story, and—see?—I have told you, a stranger, mine within a moment of meeting you. Unburdening oneself can be great catharsis, as my friends will attest." She indicated the three other young women, whose mouths all turned up in a sympathy that shone from their eyes.

Cressida stared. In harmony, they'd seemed as one, but now that they'd drawn closer and the candlelight flickered across their features, she saw the tallest was crowned with a cascade of jet black hair as glossy as a raven's wing, her sharp, pretty little face viewing Cressida with fixed interest. The other two were fair, the youngest of them rubbing swollen eyes, suggesting she'd just been crying.

"If you heard our stories," Ariane said softly, "you'd realize you were little different from the rest of us and that we are here, like you, looking for the same thing — love."

"I have love," Cressida said woodenly, looking from their four earnest faces to the dim, ordinary room beyond. "I have a loving husband at home."

The women exchanged looks which made Cressida cringe inside though she fought the urge to add emphasis to her statement.

"Except that you think he's here, and that's why you've bravely set out to search for him. You think he's been taking pleasure in a house like this," Ariane paused meaningfully, adding, "with women like us."

Cressida shook her head. "No, I'm sure he'd never—"

"Nor would we, for we are not lightskirts who sell our bodies for the pleasure of men," said the youngest woman fiercely, dabbing her eyes with her chiffon scarf as she broke away from the comfort of her companions to confront Cressida. "Though often one's body is the only commodity we have, and selling it is the only way to stop from starving when a woman has no man to support her." Her voice trembled. "So we dance, and while we are young and still have our looks, men pay for the pleasure of watching us. We're not forced to do anything we don't want to do at Madam Plumb's salon, for she is not like some women who run houses of ill repute and profit from defenseless women and who are just as wicked and depraved as the men who frequent these establishments. We've come to this house because Mrs. Plumb *protects* those who have been ruined by such men and women, but we are not"—she gulped—"cyprians or jades."

"You've explained that more than thoroughly enough, Minna," Ariane said, her voice sharper than Cressida had heard it as Minna started to cry and was comforted by the two other 'Vestal Virgins'.

Ariane tilted her head and said, conspiratorially, "Minna has been here nearly two years and is happy enough after the horrors she endured before. Tonight it's been a great shock for her to see the young man who once courted her and to whom she lost her heart when she was a parson's daughter in her first season out," Ariane explained. "Unlike me, who's only been taught how to play a lady when expedient, she grew up privileged in a fine house with a horse and carriage. Her fall from grace has been hard for her."

Cressida pressed her hand to her throat. She'd never met women like this. 'Ruined' women were contagious, their sin likely to contaminate the rarified purity of well-born women like Cressida. But now she was talking to them, her own subterfuge and disguise lessening the chasm between them and blurring the lines of distinction. She was shocked to find how drawn she was to them.

"Then why is she here?" she whispered.

"Because she was ruined on her first visit to the capital to stay with her godmother in Mayfair," said the red-haired Vestal Virgin sadly, extricating herself from Minna's side and draping an arm around Cressida's shoulders. "During a shopping expedition, she lost her way when she paused to look into a street window and then found her godmother gone. Being such an innocent, she had no idea of the danger she courted when she accepted the invitation of a seemingly kind and elderly woman to take refreshment while a boy was supposedly dispatched to take a message to Minna's aunt. This woman happened to procure girls for Mrs. Saville's brothel in Soho. Now Minna is ruined and she can never go home."

Ariane corroborated the redhead's story with a nod. "It's a sad tale, Persephone, indeed it is, with no happy ending in sight, for poor Minna has ever spoken with longing of this Mr. de Courtney, her young man whom she saw tonight, three years after her ambitious mama forced her to reject his marriage offer. She thinks he may have recognized her, and she's ashamed and fears he may tell her parents, whom she hopes simply believe her dead."

"But it wasn't her fault," Cressida stammered, before realizing that it was always the woman's fault.

"No, it wasn't her fault, but that's no defense, and now Minna must earn her daily bread, as must we all and, if she's lucky, find a little love along the way before she is old and dies in the gutter."

Shocked at the harshness of Ariane's tone, Cressida reflected on her own good fortune. Regardless of whether Justin strayed or not, she was protected by his name and his wealth. She might die lonely and unhappy, but at least it would not be in a gutter.

"Surely this young man might rescue her?" she asked, realizing at the same time how absurd the notion was, for if Minna was no longer a virgin, she was indeed condemned to a lonely and miserable future with only the protection she could procure herself.

Ariane turned the subject, her voice sympathetic and questioning as she laid two hands upon Cressida's shoulders. "And why, *exactly*, are you here? You are looking for your husband? Well, there are peepholes that will give you access to many of the rooms here, though if he does not wish to be spied upon, he has that right. Many here, however, are quite happy to flaunt themselves."

"Spy? Goodness, no! I just want—"

Ariane's gentle squeeze stilled her. "You don't know what you want, I think. Or perhaps you just want to go home. This is not the place to be when you have somewhere else to go to that offers you comfort and security." She led her to the door and pointed down the corridor. "The entrance is that way. I shall be going in a different direction, for I came here to enjoy myself"—a secretive smile curved her lips—"with my friends, since I'm rarely in a position to enjoy my husband, though he *is* visiting tonight. He is very handsome, you will have noticed. Come." She started for the door and beckoned Cressida to follow. "You're very welcome to join Minna and Persephone and Julia and me, but I think perhaps you'd prefer the safety of your own bed."

Ariane left her then, brushing past her and into the passage, her companions following, and heading in the direction opposite to that in which she'd pointed Cressida.

Torn by indecision, Cressida watched them until they were nearly out of sight. Yes, she should go home. That's what she'd intended. But she'd not found Justin. She'd not begun to understand what might have drawn him to such a place—if there was any grain of truth in Catherine's words. And Ariane's own story, and that of Minna, needled her. No, Justin would never come here, but he should know of what went on, and Cressida should make him *do* something...though changing the world and a judgmental society was hardly something that could be done overnight. However, Justin was in a position of power. He *was* a man who changed the ways of the world, and wasn't that what her own papa had grown up lamenting was needed to his unworldly daughter? He always said it was a harsher world with a greater divide between the fortunate and the unfortunate than should be the case.

Justin need not know she'd been here, but he should know what terrible things happened to defenseless women unaided or even persecuted by the law. He *should* try to do his part to change the society that governed so many cruel attitudes.

Emboldened by an unexpected sense of crusade, Cressida picked up her skirts and quickly followed the young women.

She might not have much experience of the seamier side of life, but as a parson's daughter, she had not always enjoyed the sumptuous privilege she did now.

Perhaps some good could come out of this visit. For the first time Cressida felt a streak of the crusader take root inside her.

She was not going to go home just yet. There were things she had to learn, first.

CHAPTER 5

Down twisting corridors and up a shallow flight of stairs Cressida went, through a large, empty space lined with huge, lurid paintings of shocking scenes that made her gasp and avert her eyes. Then finally through a pair of carved double doors and into a room filled with soft music and a strange, unidentifiable scent overlaying the hint of rosewater.

Raising her veil once more, Cressida tried to adjust to the dimness of her new environment. When she saw that the room was sparsely furnished and contained only Ariane and her three companions, she felt no fear, and even a great sense of sisterhood, for the four of them were in the midst of a gentle, swaying dance, smiling at one another as if they shared a joyful bond.

A great weightless settled on Cressida's shoulders; as if she were somehow part of this sisterhood solidarity.

As she moved into the shadows of a huge, luxuriant potted palm to watch, an unknown, heady scent filled her nostrils making her head swim. Ariane and Minna, dressed in their flowing robes of white, did indeed look like a pair of Vestal Virgins in a trance as they swayed gently in time to their soft chanting. Their hair, held back by silver fillets, fell in loose ripples around their waists, and their smiles were warm and gentle.

Though the environment was strange, like she'd never before experienced, Cressida felt a sense of comfort and safety. Even belonging. She was amongst other women. Young and beautiful women who shared her fears, but at this elemental level, also shared a bond which united them. They looked after one another when they were all similarly vulnerable. Minna's story and the comfort and sympathy the others had shown her demonstrated that.

How different from the relationship Cressida shared with Catherine. Not only was Catherine her cousin, she was, supposedly, Cressida's closest female companion. Who else did Cressida share her fears and concerns with?

The few moments she'd spent in the company of these women made her realise there was no sense of shared purpose or sisterly bond between her and Catherine. No, Catherine was spiteful and jealous, never happier than when she could erode Cressida's confidence so she could triumph over the parson's daughter who had married so well.

The revelation was as painful as the fact that she and Justin had never been further apart than they were now, despite living side by side, united by four active children.

A rapid, low drumming noise filled the vacuum left by the music which has ceased. Cressida watched, mesmerised, as the raven-haired beauty stepped forward and linked her hands behind Ariane's neck then kissed her, ever so softly, upon the lips.

Good lord, did women do that? Cressida craned forward and saw the young woman's pale blue eyes appeared slightly unfocused. Yet she looked so supremely at peace with her world that Cressida longed to learn her secret. How could she step out of her body like that? Was it the music? The sisterly bond?

She glanced around her, unsure if she should step forward and declare herself, for though she had been invited she'd slipped, unnoticed, into the room.

Fearing she'd break the mood or spell that seemed to have everyone in its thrall, she decided against it. Instead, incredulous, she took in the surreal scene: two women gently cradling each other before pressing themselves closer to deepen their kiss.

They had come here to give themselves—to enjoy themselves beyond the realm of men. Cressida had never imagined women sharing such intimacy. Was this giving themselves up to pleasure—without a man—sanctioned as a means of finding...what? Plugging that gaping hole inside oneself when there were no words or actions that could stem the pain?

When she imagined doing any such thing with Catherine, her mind closed up and her body revolted. No, the only person she would ever want to enjoy such closeness with was Justin.

But she couldn't. Not without repercussions.

The reflection filled her with such deep sadness her legs felt weak and she wanted to weep on the spot.

When she had last experienced true uninhibited and carefree enjoyment. Of the kind these women were sharing?

Too long ago to remember. And yet, there'd been so many wonderful occasions when, beneath the covers of the marital bed in the warmth of her chamber, Justin's hard body had covered her own and he'd rained gentle kisses upon her; whipping up the kinds of responses from her that were wild and wonderful and completely unfeigned and which had so pleased him.

From the first night of marriage, Cressida had never been afraid of the act that she'd been warned by Catherine and the other women in her family it was her duty to stoically endure.

Stoically endure? What were they talking about, she'd wondered as her love for Justin took such an extraordinary turn from sensations she'd understood were restricted to the heart.

During one awkward, truncated conversation two days before she'd walked down the aisle, her aunt had hinted at what she must expect from her husband when she shared his bed. Sacrificing her body—since as the vessel that would carry the future heir under-pinned the marriage contract—was implicit in this notion of 'her duty', she gathered. What this sacrifice actually entailed was explained in confusing and oblique terms, but it would consist of some rather crude fumbling beneath the covers followed by a painful and uncomfortable penetration of her nether regions. Thus were children created and Cressida's role as wife and future mother of the next earl of Lovett cemented, her existence justified.

Catherine, newly married herself, by then, had certainly not put the gloss on matters.

"Don't be taken in by what your new husband does to try and make things less unpleasant for you, Cressy, for men are men," Catherine had said. "You'll think his kisses, and all the rest of it, are sincere—and so will he at the time—but then his interest will wane. After that, he'll take what he wants without a thought for making it less unpleasant for you." (For Cressida had hinted to her cousin her distress over the confusing conversation with her aunt.) "The worst part for you won't be what happens in the bedroom," Catherine had gone on gloomily, "but what happens in your mind."

But when Cressida had got married she'd not been able to assimilate a word of their dire pronouncements with the reality of her blissful experiences in the marital chamber.

Continually, she'd been at pains to not cry out her pleasure. To admit to such ecstasy in view of what her aunt had said the act was all about, seemed wrong and sinful. Only when she discovered that her pleasure pleased Justin, did she end the charade, and those first couple of years of intimacy between herself and her adored husband had been the most wonderful of her life.

Well after the first glow of rapture might have been expected to have dimmed, Cressida had revelled in her husband's tender ministrations. The glorious wantonness Justin managed to stir up inside her was the prelude to an endless series of shattering climaxes that preceded the peace and contentedness that always soothed her into sleep, Justin's warm, loving breath on her neck.

Now, watching the women's shared loving intimacy on stage was like opening the curtains on a new landscape.

Cressida drew in another shuddering breath, her body alive,

nerve endings prickling the surface of her skin, a desperate, throbbing ache building between her legs as she remembered those halcyon days with Justin. If only she could return home tonight and offer up her body to his tender ministrations with no danger of what was likely to happen in nine months. If only she could surrender herself to his sweet touch, enjoying to the full his expert exploration of her body. It might have been ten months since they'd shared a bed but she was ever alive to his ability to create those shattering sensations that stunned her with their intensity at night. It was true that in the morning she was often ashamed that she, a matron with so many children, should revel in those bodily sensations so divorced from the realities of procreation.

She longed for them now but couldn't talk of either her longing or her fears with Justin. That was the dreadful, painful reality.

But she could feast her eyes watching a two women enjoying a world full of love and beauty with no guilt, no terrible consequences. No conception, no pregnancy, no pain.

The women had not broken their kiss. Gently they swayed in time to the rhythm of the faint music, running their hands over each other's face and body, caressing breasts and hips as if they were the most natural of gestures.

Cressida wondered why she wasn't appalled.

All at once the tempo changed. Alertness pulsed through her as she sensed the sudden tense awareness between the women as they stepped apart, and she strained to see what was happening. The faint chanting rose to a crescendo then suddenly ceased, and from the shadows in the corner of the room strode a man, splendidly built, she observed, as a faint light burnished his statuesque silhouette. Cressida drew in her breath, embarrassed by her own response to the muscled physique and confident bearing of someone seemingly so splendid. She ran her clammy over her skirts while the back of her neck prickled as she thought of Justin and how she would feel if it were he advancing toward her.

The awe and admiration of her companions was similar as the

four women drew together, arms linked as they gazed at this being who seemed to command such power.

The haze cleared a little, both in Cressida's mind and in the room, though her head still swam with a sense of unreality. One of the women—Minna, she saw—broke away and disappeared into the shadows, returning to place three lighted candles on either side of what Cressida now saw was a large bed that thad been pushed into the center of the room, adorned with carved wooden posts and sheets of crisp, white linen. The man stood behind this on a raised dais and he beckoned to the women.

"I have returned." His voice was low and mellifluous, and as Cressida strained to see more, she recognized him as the man who'd frightened her in the corridor. Ariane's husband.

"Yes... Come to us at last." Ariane sounded breathless and her face was shining as she pushed back her flowing golden hair. She made her way toward him, climbing what Cressida assumed must be a set of stairs hidden behind the bed. The stranger caught her to his muscled chest, sliding one hand up behind her neck, the other slowly caressing the contours of her body. With a soft groan, Ariane went slack, and he whisked her up into his arms and placed his mouth upon hers.

"I offer myself up to your pleasure," whispered the red-haired siren, and she moved forward and up the stairs, kneeling to kiss his feet, her hands twining up the thick muscles of his legs.

Cressida remained rooted to the spot in shocked fascination. What was happening? The man was kissing Ariane while the other beauty was kissing his feet. No! Shock galvanized Cressida. This must be a dream. A lust-crazed dream for—Good God!—the haze was clearing, and for the first time, Cressida saw that this man was completely naked, and that while he was kissing Ariane, Persephone was kissing his feet, his ankles, the backs of his knees.

Gently the man placed Ariane upon the mattress before him, rising in tandem with Persephone, locked in a swaying embrace as she twined her arms about his neck, nuzzling his earlobe while

Ariane began her own slow progress of pleasuring her husband from his feet upward.

Cressida glanced at the door. She should not be here, witnessing such a sight. The fog in her brain was clearing, highlighting the wrongness of being in the midst of a scene of such a sexual nature.

Venturing out of her hiding place, she turned at Ariane's gasp; then gasped herself to see that this magnificent creature, wearing not a stitch of clothing, was no longer like the several sculptures of naked men with which she was familiar.

No, while Ariane swept her hands all over him in a manner beyond Cressida's imaginings, her expert tongue flicking against the backs of his knees, his body was behaving in a way which Cressida had never observed with her own eyes, though she'd been aware of the changes in her own husband during the prelude to their coupling.

Shocked and fascinated, she stared at his swollen member, which had seemingly a life of its own as Persephone kissed his mouth and Ariane rose to her knees, kissing higher...

And higher...

The pleasure haze dissipated further. Cressida could not move, fascinated and horrified in equal measure as she watched Ariane gently cup the pouches beneath her husband's rampant manhood.

No, she'd never seen a man naked. Not in eight years of marriage. She'd been gently pleasured in Justin's warm, secure embrace, but always in darkness. She'd never seen her husband clad in less than his nightshirt or banyan.

The pupils of the magnificent creature in the middle of the bed dilated, and he threw back his head as Ariane, with calculated care, put her mouth to his engorged member and slowly circled it with her tongue.

So apparent was his rapture that Cressida felt her own body pulse with sensation, despite her shock.

She put her hands to her face to cover her shame.

No one seemed to register her. All eyes were on the scene in the center of the bed—eyes greedy, lascivious, wanting...

Cressida blindly took a few steps, her terror growing, yet drawn again to the stage by the sounds of rapture. This was not a sight for a gently reared woman like herself. She had to escape.

In the gloom, she thought she recognized the door through which she'd come and stumbled toward it, turning as the man groaned his pleasure.

A final glance at his glazed eyes made plain that he was enslaved by this extraordinary act. Was he a *normal* man? Of course not, so why should she be so fascinated, her mind returning to her husband's body and what he might think of such a thing.

There. The door was before her at last. Turning the brass knob, Cressida staggered into the corridor, gasping for air. She had spied on two women kissing. She'd been unable to tear her eyes away from a naked man in the throes of passion. What had she done? Her recent fascination now seemed nothing more than wicked prurience.

She was going to be ill, she knew it. And if not, that was the reaction she ought to have. Panting, sweating, she sought desperately for the privy, which, to her relief, was pointed out to her by a motherly looking woman dressed in cerulean silk.

When Cressida returned weakly to the passage a few minutes later, her savior was waiting for her, a look of sympathetic concern upon her face.

"My dear, let me take you somewhere private where you can compose yourself."

The kindness of the woman's expression, and her thoughtfulness—so different from what she'd expected to find in a place like this—made Cressida want to burst into tears.

With a grateful nod, she allowed herself to be led into a small, private sitting room at the back of the house, where she was gently pushed down onto an Egyptian sofa. When she looked up, a handkerchief scented with Cressida's favorite lavender water was being waved in front of her face.

"My dear, I think you are out of your depth," murmured the woman as Cressida cooled her forehead and dabbed the corners of her trembling mouth. "Shall I order a carriage to take you home?"

Go home? Cressida shook her head. How could she go home in this state? She was shaking like a leaf, her mind roiling with images of the naked man she'd just seen and the ecstasy he'd clearly experienced at the hands of... What was Ariane? A woman of the night? Yet she claimed she was this man's wife. Did that mean that what they shared was sanctioned by the church? Surely not? Ariane had said she was 'just like her'. Like Cressida, hinting they both were married women sharing a private sadness. No, Cressida had nothing in common with Ariane, and the sooner she was out of this place the better.

There was something ordinary and soothing about the comfortably decorated sitting room.

"Take a few deep breaths and close your eyes for a moment," said the woman. "It will make you feel much better. Now, look at me." Her smile took years off her age, her twinkling brown eyes suggesting a surprising depth of insight and intelligence for a woman who lived in such a depraved setting as this.

Cressida her lip and sank against the cushions of the sofa as images of beautiful maidens kissing each other and magnificently muscled men with rampant members chased around her brain.

Her remembered excitement made her curl up inside with guilt.

What had she done? What would Justin think if he knew she'd witnessed such a tableau and...that she'd been excited by it? He'd never look at her the same way. Never touch her...

Enough presence of mind remained for Cressida to understand the irony of such a fear. The way she was conducting herself in this marriage, Justin never *was* going to touch her.

She had to take matters into her own hands. *But how?*

"I think, my dear, you did not understand what it meant for you to come to such a place."

Cressida opened her eyes and found she was staring directly at a pair of once-elegant dancing slippers beneath a cerulean skirt.

Taking in the faded elegance of the woman's dress, the gray in her jet-black hair and the sympathy of her expression, she questioned her original assumption of this woman's calling. After all, Cressida was here, in this house, and *she* wasn't a...

A what? Her heart seemed to thud to her feet and she looked down.

After what she'd participated in, she didn't know what she was.

"Who are you—?" she began before halting at the rudeness of such blunt questioning.

"A friend of Mrs. Plumb's—you may call me Miss Mariah—and this is my drawing room, where you are welcome to remain for as long as you need to." Miss Mariah rose and came toward her, placing a gentle hand upon Cressida's shoulder. The sensation that swept over her was completely different to her reaction to Mrs. Plumb. Everything about this woman was motherly. Unthreatening.

"Now, perhaps a little medicinal brandy?" Miss Mariah suggested, moving to a small table by a bookshelf. "You're shaking like a leaf, and it'll be an aid to unburdening yourself of your troubles, if nothing else. You would not be in this house with such a look in your eyes if you were free of fear or troubles."

"Thank you," Cressida managed through chattering teeth as she accepted a glass. Miss Mariah was right. She was out of her depth, amongst a sophisticated, worldly, *depraved* crowd—with whom she had nothing in common. In this cheaply decorated house of ill repute, witty conversation and good music were enjoyed and physical attractions acted upon through discreet assignations.

Oh, dear Lord. A fresh tremor of guilt wracked her as she was revisited by the sensations that had gripped her when she'd watched the four lovely women. Envy. Envy that they could enjoy gentle loving without fear of the repercussions. But worse was her reaction when she'd watched Ariane pleasure the man on the bed.

She'd been speared with excitement and, yes, lust as she'd gazed upon the scene and registered the pleasure with which he received Ariane's ministrations.

Was it possible such things happened in the intimacy of the marital bedroom, too? Justin had never indicated in all their private moments together that there was anything missing in their relations. That there might be more and different acts of pleasure beyond the enjoyable, predictable buildup of sensation she felt prior to his plunging into her.

Planting his seed and leaving her with the consequences. She gasped. *Where had such a wicked, disloyal thought come from?*

Her companion touched her cheek and, dazed, Cressida looked up into her compassionate eyes.

"Guilt will not help." Miss Mariah's look was knowing. "When a woman like you comes to this house, she usually has a good reason."

Cressida thought of all the other people who'd come to this house. People driven here by their lustful, depraved impulses to find release in sinful pleasures of the flesh. Driven here through... With devastating clarity, truth limned the conclusion of her observation. *Driven here through desperation, when the domestic arena failed to satisfy.*

She gasped.

Was it any surprise Justin had felt the need to stray? What pleasures did his wife offer him since she had denied him her body? She'd even stopped being affectionate except in the company of the children, too afraid her overtures may lead to the bedroom.

She was dimly conscious of the clink of glass before a second measure of brandy was placed into her hands. And then the question, a gentle enquiry that unleashed a torrent of emotion: "Would you like to tell me who you are looking for?"

How quickly the tears flowed. Wiping her face with the back of her hand, Cressida cursed her frail nerves. The past few months seemed to see her lurch from one emotional episode to another.

"My husband," she whispered through her fingers as she hunched over, covering her face. "I heard he attends Mrs. Plumb's salons and that he's"—she sucked in a shaky breath—"taken a mistress." What did it matter that her dreadful fears were revealed to this stranger? A kind stranger with a motherly touch. Cressida was too distraught for caution. "At first, I didn't believe it. No." She drew herself up straight and fixed a defiant stare upon Miss Mariah. "I *don't* believe it. Not my husband, who's shown me nothing but kindness, respect and affection since we met. And yet—"

The specter of what the unknown man in the room beyond had come for, and why—taking his pleasures like an arrogant young god—continued to haunt her. Was that what the men who came here indulged in? Did it really give them pleasure? Cressida had never touched her husband intimately with more than a fleeting, half-accidental caress. She'd allowed him to take control, and although their lovemaking had been wonderful, she'd never in a million years dreamed of taking the initiative in such wanton exploration.

The very idea made her squirm with embarrassment at the same time as her body burned with a slow, intense heat.

She shifted position, unable to look Miss Mariah in the eye.

"You must love your husband very much to come to a place like this if you are the innocent you appear to be," remarked her new friend. "I think you are very brave."

"Or very stupid," sniffed Cressida looking at her and feeling the truth of her words lie heavily upon her shoulders. "If I'd been a better wife, he'd never have strayed, would he?"

"How like a woman to blame oneself. If your husband has strayed, *who* has committed the sin?"

Cressida stilled. She'd never thought of it in those terms. Then guilt, a far more loyal companion than she was a wife, washed over her as she blurted out the truth. "The fault is mine since it is I who have denied him his rights."

"I believe it is an obligation for a husband to learn how to please his wife sufficiently so she does not object so strenuously to doing what the marriage act requires." Miss Mariah smiled. "There, what a revolutionary notion and yet, anything else is barbarism, surely?" She sighed. "Young women are brought up in ignorance. Yet it is called innocence and it is nurtured. A travesty!" Clearly, Miss Mariah had strong feelings on the subject. Stoutly, she declared, "The fault lies not with the innocent wife but with the husband. You should not fear what is only natural between a man and a woman. An act that can bind two hearts together and underpin a life together of love and tenderness. Very few enjoy such happiness...and yet, it *is* possible."

"My husband is one of the kindest and most loving men I know," Cressida defended him, distraught at having suggested Tristan was anything but.

"You are a loyal wife." Clearly Miss Mariah misinterpreted Cressida for she went on, "But it is far from unusual for a husband to use the marital chamber for the duties of marriage and to take his pleasures elsewhere." She patted Cressida's arm. "You came here to find your husband but perhaps here you will find pleasure, also. Everyone deserves that."

"It's not the pleasure but the consequences!" Cressida blurted out.

It was as if a sudden silence descended upon the room. Cressida tensed, shocked at the force of her desperation and the fact she'd admitted it at all; that not only had she admitted to pleasure but that pleasure's *consequences* were at the heart of her reluctance to be a good wife. No, a *dutiful* wife.

The woman put her head on one side, her look of enquiry a potent offering that Cressida unburden herself. But Cressida had gone too far. Her moral fibre was a mere thread and to say more would see even that unravelling. Then what would be left of her?

"I must go." She started to rise but Miss Mariah stayed her with a hand on her wrist.

"My dear, you've only just begun. Stay. It's the reason you came here. Not only to find your husband but to understand for yourself the source of your torment."

Cressida sank into her chair again and stared at Miss Mariah. The kindly eyes, the air of safety and lack of judgement she exuded were having a potent effect on her. Whom else could she confide in. And what would be the harm? She certainly couldn't hint to Justin that was her *obligation* that drained the joy from her marriage. Not only would that brand her a failure as a wife but as a good, decent and upstanding woman in the eyes of the church and of society. It was all Cressida had ever been trained for.

So, feeling her shoulders slump and staring first at Miss Mariah and then at an incongruous painting of Christ upon the cross that hung behind her left shoulder, she said, "Mama died giving birth to my brother, her sixth child. I've had four children in less than eight years..."

She knew her situation was not unusual. Many women had more within that amount of time so why was she complaining? She stopped. It was as if a wellspring of emotion had been tapped. Having started so well, she could now barely get the words out as she hunched over, speaking between sobs. "Each year, I have another child, and each time, it's been harder. I cannot bear it anymore. I need a rest, yet until this moment, I couldn't even put my fear into words. No wonder my husband is hurt and confused and—" she gulped, "needing diversion." For as she said the words, she allowed in just a little more doubt. Justin was the kindest of men and she knew he loved her, but of course even the very best of men needed physical release in a way women did not. Would it be so very surprising if he had come to Mrs. Plumb's seeking what he could not get at home? Had Cressida any right to despise him if he did? She'd made it so clear she no longer embraced her conjugal duties, yet not once had Justin pressed her. She should take the fact he discreetly visited a house of assignation as a sign of his consideration for her and leave it at that. Be satisfied.

But satisfied she was not, and wasn't that just another reason for her being nothing but a spoiled, cosseted wife who failed to appreciate the great bounties she'd been given.

She glanced at Miss Mariah, disappointed, though not surprised, to see the shock on her face.

Obviously this woman thought Cressida gravely remiss, too. Quickly, she rose, wrinkling her nose at the smell of cheap perfume and staring at the faded, drawn curtains, wondering if the moon was out and how fast she could be back in the safety of her own home. The room suddenly seemed tawdry and her own little soul dried up and shrivelled. "I'm wicked, I know! You have every right to look at me like I've failed my duty. I know what I must do now. I have to win him back. I have to be the wife he wants and needs." She only realized how hard she'd been shaking when the woman put her hands on her shoulders to push her back down into her seat. Despite her urgency to leave, Cressida welcomed the comfort in the gesture, the soothing smile. It had been a long time since she'd welcomed a comforting touch. She daren't risk it with Justin. But her resolve was stronger than ever. Closing her eyes, she whispered through clenched teeth, "Even if it kills me."

"My poor child. Surely you don't think I condemn you for such an understandable fear." Her companion's words had the comfort of a caress as she deflected blame away from Cressida. And suddenly hope was let in like a ray of sun into her dark, dull mind.

She opened her eyes and stared. Waiting for more. "If you only knew how easy it was to be helped, and yet women like you are kept in ignorance. Truly, you may hold your husband in thrall, or submit, or whatever it is that makes you feel you're doing your duty, but please understand there is no reason for you to make *sacrifices*."

In all her life, Cressida had never discussed the intimacies of marriage. To be able to do so now with a stranger felt like a great weight had been lifted from her shoulders. She raised hopeful eyes. This woman didn't think Cressida a disloyal wife? *No reason to make sacrifices?*

Her companion cleared her throat, as if understanding the delicacy her approach required for one of Cressida's innocence and ignorance. She rose, smoothing her cerulean skirts as she began to pace, biting her lip as if she were contemplating a great conundrum. Cressida followed her with her eyes, tense to hear what she might say.

Miss Mariah turned in the window embrasure. "Lord knows, it's important enough, but preventing conception is a sin to some and for the rest, not a subject considered appropriate talk between husbands and wives of your station." She raised her eyes heavenward as if she had her own thoughts on that subject before turning back to look at Cressida. "It would be safe to assume you have not asked your husband to take precautions?"

Cressida gasped. She felt shocked, outraged and embarrassed in equal measure. "Precautions?" For a moment, she grappled with the meaning, much less the concept. "How could I—?"

Smiling, her friend sighed. "Of course not," she said, grasping the curtain edge. "It is a conversation a man has with his mistress, not his wife. I daresay you do not even know wet nursing your child will lessen the likelihood of conception."

What words were these? Cressida had no knowledge of the way such matters worked. She'd barely thought to question what she knew would not be forthcoming. A woman's duty was set in stone and that was that. She frowned and shook her head. "I wanted very much to suckle my children myself," she said, remembering the pain of the various conversations she'd had with the women in her family. Older women who had strong views on the subject. "My mother-in-law told me it was not the role of a woman in my position. She found me a wet nurse, a healthy, kind woman, who has nursed all my children, including little Thomas, our only son, a sickly child who needs all my care." Her voice broke. "I should be with him now."

"Little Thomas no doubt has a devoted nursemaid. But, my dear, abstinence is not the only answer. If you still harbor such a *tendre* for your husband, surely he is sufficiently in tune with your feelings to have remarked upon your withdrawal from the usual intimacies?"

They had ventured too far for Cressida to feel embarrassed. It was even a relief for her to relive her awful exchange with Justin some months before, and again just after, Lady Belton's ball. "My husband did ask me," she managed, twisting her hands in her lap, "after yet another of my excuses, whether I was afraid of conceiving a child."

There was a pause. "And your reply?"

Miserably, Cressida admitted, "I adamantly denied it—"

"Good Lord, child, why? Not every husband shows such a capacity for understanding."

Even now, Cressida couldn't quite understand her reasons, though though of course it had been fueled by fear and obedience as always. Four nights ago had been no different. "Before we married, my mother-in-law told me it was my duty never to question my husband and to deny him nothing. My own family made a point of telling me how fortunate I was that I'd been elevated to such heights and that as a poor parson's daughter I must *always* submit else I'd bring shame upon them and upon the great name my children would inherit. Little Thomas is our only son, and being such a sickly child, I was reminded that my chief duty was to ensure *more* sons in the nursery."

"But not every year! How many children did you say you had?"

"Four living. A child for almost every year we've been married for several did not reach full term. The last birth was very difficult." She shuddered at the memory. "When he was only a few months old, I started making excuses to my husband each time he —" Dabbing at the fresh tears that ran down her cheeks, Cressida stood up. "What else can I say? I've admitted it all! I was a fool to come here. I have friends who have nurseries larger than mine and, no doubt, far more satisfied husbands, so of course mine is perfectly justified—"

"Stop!" Arresting her retreat with a stern frown, her friend went on. "You say you love your husband."

"I *adore* him—"

"Yet you cannot speak to him of your fears?"

"What do wives know of such things?" Despairingly, Cressida continued, supporting herself with a hand on the back of the sofa as she started towards the door. "My mother died when I was a child. Whom can I ask? No one told me what to expect on my wedding night, much less—" Taking a deep, sustaining breath, she calmed herself. "Do you have children?" she suddenly asked.

Her new friend certainly inferred that she knew a lot more about minimizing their likelihood than Cressida did. And she must be 'experienced', otherwise she'd not be here.

She thought Miss Mariah had not heard, for she appeared distracted as she fiddled with the tassels of the brocade curtain. "No," came the answer, eventually, and much to Cressida's surprise.

"But you've had lovers?" Cressida heard the desperate note in her voice, as if pleading for the two to be compatible. How pathetic she must seem. This was a fool's errand. "I'm sorry. That was impolite of me." She clasped her reticule against her and took another step toward the door.

"Home, to your children?" A smile hovered about Miss Mariah's mouth as she fixed Cressida with a level stare. "Or to find your husband and explain what is at the root of your troubles? If he is as considerate as it would appear, I think your frankness will not go unrewarded."

Cressida winced. "My youngest is teething—" she mumbled.

"With a competent nursery maid. I'll wager your husband needs you more. Listen to me. I know all about husbands, too. I was married for many years, and I can assure you that husbands and lovers are no different where a desirable woman is concerned." With an incisive look she asked, "I am curious. If you *had* found your husband here, in the arms of his mistress, do you think your feelings for him would survive the trauma? Yes, I know straying husbands are a matter of course, but it is easier to ignore and forgive what is not presented to you on a platter."

Through gritted teeth, Cressida maintained what she truly

believed. "I will *always* love him, for if he'd strayed, I'd know it was only because I'd driven him to it."

She'd reached the door and now turned, hurt and angered by the smile on Miss Mariah's face. "You think it's not true? I've had time to reflect, and I've been reminded of my duty. Women like me have no choice but to be compliant wives if we want to trade in happiness. I am going home to wait for my husband and to do whatever is required so that he will *never* seek diversion elsewhere. I shall return to reclaim his heart." Lowering the veil of her bonnet, she put out her hand. "You have been patient, listening to my foolishness. You talk of sacrifices not being required, but I am not—" She swallowed. "That kind of woman. Women like me must honor our marriage vows in return for comfort and security. We have an obligation to our husbands, and I'm about to fulfill mine, though, truly, I thank you for your good advice." She pushed away Miss Mariah's restraining hand to turn the doorknob, but it was the woman's soft, suggestive words that proved too intriguing to resist.

"It is not your husband's heart that needs repossessing but his desire. Of course you are upset, my dear, but think a moment on the reasons you came here...of your fears and what I can teach you." She came up close behind Cressida and put her hand on her shoulder. Then gently she touched her cheek.

The gesture of sympathy was almost more than Cressida could bear, but she had to leave before she succumbed to the fresh wave of self-pity that threatened to overcome her. She turned the door handle.

"I would be very happy to stay, my dear. But if you're intent upon leaving, don't, I implore you, act with too much haste and undo all the good that's come from your bravery tonight."

Cressida turned as Miss Mariah put a hand on Cressida's shoulder, then tucked an escaped tendril behind her ear. "I would be very happy if you would like to come back next Wednesday so I can tell you more about the many women *like you* who do not have extensive nurseries but who are equally dutiful wives. For if you return, I can show you how to satisfy your husband without necessarily conceiving a child."

Cressida stilled. This was the second time the woman had alluded to such a possibility, but the first she'd said it in such direct words.

"Satisfy my husband without conceiving a child." She repeated the phrase, more as an incantation than questioning the assertion. What a incongruous notion. And yet...a tremor of hope and excitement started at the core of her.

Her friend gripped Cressida's fingertips and gave a comforting squeeze. "That's what women do when they're not raised in fear and ignorance."

CHAPTER 6

S he'd learned nothing, yet she'd learned too much to go home and meekly await Justin's return. Excitement thrummed through Cressida's veins as she stepped out of Miss Mariah's sitting room and into the dimly lit corridor. Quickly she lowered her head as two passersby approached. A smirking young man was holding up a woman old enough to be his mother, whose drunken laughter and unsteady gait sent them on a trajectory that required Cressida to press herself against the wall for fear of being bowled over.

Lord, she thought, panic gripping her as she touched her thick veil for reassurance, ducking into an alcove to tidy her hair so it was completely concealed by the ugly bonnet. What would Justin say if he discovered her in such a place? His faith in her constancy as a pliant, loving wife would be rocked to the core. Could he even look at her in the same way, knowing what she must have seen simply by coming here?

Yet what she'd gained was inestimable. Hope and courage and the curiosity to find the answers to what she'd once thought an insoluble problem.

Yet, if what Miss Mariah said was true, Cressida might, in a few days' time, have all the knowledge she needed to return her and Justin to the glorious days when they'd reveled in their newly wedded bliss. What power that would be!

Entering through a doorway at the end of the corridor, such revolutionary thoughts were, in only a few minutes, giving sway to a fresh wave of doubts. But she forced herself to concentrate on the hope she now embraced rather than the guilt and shame that would stifle her if she let it. She must put it out of her mind. Never hint to Justin what she'd seen—

With sudden disorientation, she realized that what she'd believed to be the hallway when she issued through the door was instead another private sitting room, cozily furnished with a fire crackling in the grate. In the far corner was a desk lit by an Argand lamp, at which sat a gentleman bent over a document he was reading. His frown indicated the deepest concentration, his left hand thrumming his knee, his right foot tapping as if he was agitated. Like everyone else here this evening, he was dressed in masquerade, a demi-mask half covering his face that he must have forgotten to remove, considering no one else occupied the room. The pristine spill of his cravat was the only relief to his austere clothing, which was cut to perfection and which clung to him...

In the most heart-stopping way.

Heart-stopping because this was just how Justin had affected Cressida the very first time she had met him, when he'd bent to kiss her hand as he'd asked her to stand up with him for the next country dance.

The sight of the man slowly raising his head, warm brown eyes regarding her with unmistakable interest, sucked the air from her lungs, a reaction as piercing now as it was a whole eight years and so much history ago.

"Oh!" she gasped as she raked her gaze over the familiar masculine form. His relaxed and pleasant smile lent him an air of calm and dignified authority. And safety.

Then terror washed over Cressida, that all her wickedness was about to be revealed.

What could she say that would adequately explain her presence? Dear Lord, she'd been caught. Either she was sneaking after him as if she didn't trust him, or she was the kind of depraved being who sought out the sins of the flesh in a place like this. What kind of a wife would he think her? Mistrustful? Deceitful? Depraved?

She closed her eyes and forced herself to be calm. She could barely see clearly through the thickness of her veil.

Of course he has no idea who I am.

"Madam?" He raised his eyebrows in polite inquiry, and her resolve shattered. Her husband was smiling at her and every particle of her being answered in a breathless chorus—anything to be in his arms. He was the breath of her life, the sun to her moon, the axis on which her existence revolved. He was the reason she was here, so that she might rediscover the secret of the happiness they once had shared.

"Sir." On sudden impulse, she swallowed down her fear, forcing a smile as calm and self-controlled as his as she closed the door behind her. Here was her beloved husband, whose heart she believed she still possessed, but whose desire she was desperate to rekindle...if what her new friend had told her was true—that passion and pregnancy need not always go hand in hand.

Justin was busy working at something. She knew that his look of polite interest masked the fact that his mind was completely on his task.

He was here...alone. There was a document in his hands. Not a woman.

And he had no idea who his new visitor was. Cressida could say anything, do anything...

The sense of being an actress in a play took hold. Boldly, she went over to him, standing in his light, just a couple of feet away.

Now his smile was distant and there was a slight wariness in his tone as he murmured, "I think you have lost your way, madam, for the front door is down the corridor to your right. Shall I show you the way?"

She did not move, did not falter as she gazed up at him through her heavy veil. Justin was here at Mrs. Plumb's, exactly where she'd dreaded she'd find him, but her heart and mind could only rejoice in the fact that his concentration on a particular document suggested his interest in the place was not the women.

Of course it was not, and how like Justin. Justin was just as likely to be concerned over the use of child labor as the rescue of fallen women. That must be why he was here. On work matters, yet he'd not wanted to hint to his protected wife that such business involved him with the depraved creatures who inhabited Madame Plumb's.

With all Cressida's doubts about Justin's constancy dissipated, she found herself now trembling with the unadulterated joy at the prospect of being taken in the arms of her wonderful, noble, *constant* husband once again.

Yet as she stepped forward, she felt again the slightest stirring of doubt. Catherine always told her she was much too credulous for her own good.

"Mrs. Plumb told me I'd find the gentleman I was looking for in *this* room." She made her voice softer, breathier. Gripping her reticule against her chest for courage, she stared at him through her veil, striving for a tone and gesture both appealing and vulnerable. Justin's chivalrous impulses were easily stirred. She wanted to see the effect she had on him when she was not his wife, but a stranger. An appealing, interested stranger.

"I am a widow, sir. I lost my beloved husband a year ago. Mrs. Plumb directed me here. She said you were a kind man who'd listen...if I wanted to talk."

Despite the dimness of the room, she saw indecisiveness cross his face. Justin *was* a kind man, but how far would he allow himself to be swayed by a lonely widow? How much did she want him to be?

She caught herself up. Took a step backwards. This was madness. She had no desire to be confronted by her husband's weaknesses—if he had any—yet here they were, in a cozy, intimate setting, where each could pretend to be someone else.

It was too much to resist.

Lowering herself onto the sofa, she tilted her head in invitation. "Just five minutes of your time, sir. Perhaps you knew my husband?"

❁

JUSTIN WAS ON THE POINT OF REFUSING, OF KINDLY BUT FIRMLY leading the woman out of the sitting room, when his senses switched to high alert. There was something familiar about the line of her throat when she tilted her head, glimpsed for a second through her thick veil. Also, the voice—the soft, breathy tone could almost be...

When she stepped from the shadows and into the light, he thought he was hallucinating.

Why, Cressida would no more frequent a place like this than have a public affair with the footman.

Yet the doubt refused to be dislodged. Frowning, Justin cautiously seated himself beside her as he was bid. It was impossible to make out her features, but the slender line of her body beneath the black silk gown and the swell of her breasts, even more desirable after four children, were devastatingly familiar. He shook his head to clear it. He was being ridiculous. It was wishful thinking or his worst nightmare.

The sofa was small and he sat awkwardly, his thigh touching hers. If it was, in fact, Cressida, he acknowledged wryly, then this tableau promised greater intimacy between them than they'd shared in many months.

Doubt dissipated when she moved slightly and a faint waft of lavender mixed with his wife's familiar scent confirmed what his sixth sense had been screaming since she'd spoken.

This was no bereaved widow wanting to lament her late husband.

He hid his confusion behind a concerned, interested smile as she created a fiction about her loss in that maddeningly sensual, familiar, breathy voice of hers. What was she about? How could his innocent, protected little Cressida be in Mrs. Plumb's house of ill repute, making up to a strange gentleman?

On the one hand, Justin wanted to leap up and declare himself —and thus force her to reveal *herself*. On the other, he wanted to tease out her reasons and so lay his torment to rest. Cressida... revealing hidden desires in a house of sin and not able to tell him?

Perhaps she *did* know it was him. And yet, the room was so dim and he'd replaced his mask. It was possible she did not. Good God, it was entirely possible she believed him someone else!

He shook his head to clear it and hurt welled up where confusion had set in. Did she no longer find him attractive now that age had set in and he was no longer the vigorous sapling of a youth he'd been when he married her? Could that be why she was seeking alternative avenues of pleasure by coming here? *Here?* To such a place? He swallowed painfully. How could she know of it? Had Catherine introduced her to it?

Then realisation and, with it, relief swept all confusion away. Of course! This was all part of the charade. She knew exactly who he was, just as she knew he realized her identity.

Cressida, who had allowed him to lie with her only once since Thomas' birth, was now here, using Mrs. Plumb's as the setting for signaling his readmittance to the marriage bed. God knew how she'd located him, but she had, though it seemed too incredible to believe, it was so out of character.

It was also unbelievably exciting. The dull ache in his loins became almost painful as he forced down his desire.

"You miss your husband, madam?" He hoped he sounded more sympathetic than hoarse with anticipation. Cressida had used this charade to initiate their physical reunion, and he was fully determined to play along.

He took her gloved hand and placed it on his knee. Her hand shook and another wave of her familiar scent assailed his nostrils, making him weak with longing. Not that he was going to remain weak for very long when given this incredible opportunity.

"I miss his love and his comfort," she whispered, her eyes fixed coyly upon their linked hands.

"So that's why you came here? To Mrs. Plumb's?" He could feel the warmth radiating from her body a hair's breadth from his and longed to offer her the love and comfort she sought with no further preliminaries. Then he'd proceed to remind her of all the other delights she'd been missing for so long.

But this was Cressida's charade. She wanted to set the pace. Desire and anticipation ratcheted up even further. Cressida could set whatever pace she wanted if it meant a resumption of the bedroom delights he missed so much. Restraint did not come easily, but he satisfied himself by reaching across and gently stroking her neck, tangling his fingers in the silky, flaxen curls at the nape as he drew her closer into his embrace. She had always liked that.

It was a successful strategy. He heard her faint intake of breath before she whispered, "I am not in the habit of frequenting such a place except that my cousin told me sometimes both ladies and gentlemen come here f-for reasons other than the music." Her voice faltered as she raised her eyes to his. "Do you come here for reasons other than the music, sir?"

He weighed up his answer, her hand captive in his. Without going into greater detail than he was prepared to at this time, he could not tell her about Mariah and the specific undertaking with which he had concerned himself on her behalf for the past three weeks. Cressida must have innocently followed him here in disguise. She certainly could not understand what went on at Mrs. Plumb's, else she'd not have made it through the front doors.

And yet...

With vivid clarity, he recalled Cressida's enthusiasm for the decorous, almost chaste lovemaking they'd enjoyed in the early days of their marriage. Had she grown bold, all of a sudden? Wished to up the pace now that she was ready to allow him access to her body at last? Why else would she bare her charms and speak so suggestively unless she knew exactly what she was about?

As to her inevitable question regarding what had brought him to Mrs. Plumb's in the first place, he'd be in a position to reveal everything within just a few days. Cressida's close friend, Annabelle Luscombe, who worked with him on the Sedleywich Board of the Foundling Home, was too closely involved and he was honor-bound to help Mariah locate her lost child first, as promised, before discreetly explaining the details to his wife.

Let Cressida assume he was in this house to examine its proximity to the river as a cause of water infection, or the possible exploitation of children—perhaps she'd think he was merely here to accompany a friend from his club.

"I enjoy the music," he said. Smiling, squeezing her hand, he added, "But tonight I prefer the company." He wanted to reassure her that he was still the same loving husband, despite her emotional and physical withdrawal, and that he was more than happy to continue her charade on her terms.

The feel of her hourglass figure beneath her widow's weeds when he discreetly skimmed her waist as he shifted position speared him with another rush of lust. The rapid rise and fall of her bosom indicated she felt as he. She tilted her head, and beneath her veil, he could just make out the curve of her lips. It was an invitation he'd never been able to resist. An invitation he'd not had from her in years, in fact.

But when he clasped her waist to draw her to him, she jerked back.

"I must go!" Her unexpected reaction shocked him. Like a frightened deer, she made an attempt to withdraw her hand and would have risen had he not pulled her back down, caging her hand on his thigh as he ground out, "I am sorry for your loss, madam, but consider me at your service." He heard the strained suggestiveness in his voice. The tone sounded alien, even to his own ears, but he was desperate that she not lose courage now.

"Let me go now, sir, and I will return here to meet you next Wednesday."

She sounded breathless and full of indecision as she pulled decisively away, smoothing her black silk skirts as she stood. He felt, rather than observed, her resolve falter and imagined her biting her lip, that adorable habit he remembered from her youth that made her dimples so gorgeously evident in her delicately tinted cheeks, though tonight he could not see behind her veil. Lord, she appeared barely older than a debutante, even now. Four beautiful children since their marriage eight years ago had only increased her womanly charms.

He let her go. Everything was in Cressida's hands now, and he was her putty. She clearly did not want to continue in this tawdry place. He imagined the seduction scene she was no doubt planning a short while hence. He'd come to her like he'd done a hundred times and still be affected by the glow of candlelight on Cressida's ivory-tinted flesh and the limpid look in her cornflower blue eyes as she gazed up at him with love and trust...

He swallowed, clenching his teeth against the fire in his loins, desperate to hold her with no barriers between them but knowing he must practice the restraint of a lifetime.

Though he rose, he did not follow her. It was clear she had reached the limit of her bravado for the moment. From the door, she hesitated, her look inquiring. "I look forward to continuing our conversation next Wednesday."

"I anticipate it very much."

With pounding heart, he watched her leave. Now she would return home. She had made her point, intimating that he should not be long in following her. The blood thrummed in his brain and he realized almost with embarrassment as he glanced down that he was as randy as a young buck. He'd thought he had more self-control, but tonight's play-acting had reinforced how much he missed their intimacy. For so long he'd pretended away his loneliness and confusion at her rejection, but now Cressida was returning to him with all the love and willingness she'd once shown him.

Heart beating wildly, Justin tidied away the half-written report he'd prepared for Mariah. In half an hour, he would be where he felt most at home—locked in Cressida's enthusiastic embrace.

CHAPTER 7

Wind whipped the branches of the tree against Cressida's bedchamber window. A storm was brewing, said Tom, the footman. He should know, for he was a farmer's son.

But Cressida was a parson's daughter, and she knew nothing about anything except what was required of her to be a good wife.

She drew the counterpane up to her chin and shivered, wishing it were with anticipation at the same time that she wished Justin were cuddled warmly against her. But that was not to be, not tonight.

At first, the limpid look in Justin's eye when he'd held her hand in that tawdry sitting room at Mrs. Plumb's had sliced away at her soul. She'd seen the hunter in him size up his quarry. At eighteen, she'd been easy prey, falling into his arms during their first waltz. There'd been no chase on Justin's part, for their hearts and minds had been as one from the start.

He'd quickly realized it was his wife, though, in that shabby little sitting room in that wicked house. She knew Justin too well. His sudden stillness and the change in his tone had alerted her to the fact that he knew exactly who she was.

Without missing a beat, he'd continued the charade while her brain had been in a whirl as to whether to admit her identity. Yet when Justin so willingly endorsed their play-acting, the exciting possibilities had quickly taken on a life of their own.

He'd agreed to an assignation a week hence. Her body pulsed at the thought before fear intruded that he'd come to her too soon. How could she hold him at bay? In a week, she'd have all the tools and knowledge she needed to be everything Justin could desire. Miss Mariah had promised.

But she didn't have them now. She was as ignorant of the practicalities as she'd ever been, though at least she now knew that precautions were possible.

Of course, her kindly friend at Mrs. Plumb's would advise her to explain everything to Justin. But how could Cressida tell him everything? That she was afraid of giving him another child? Another son? Panic banished reason. All she wanted was one more week—then she'd be all-powerful in her knowledge. Miss Mariah could help her with the words she needed to explain that she was not abrogating her childbearing duty, she just wanted to be in control of it. It was a treasonous sentiment, and there must be more artful ways for a wife to communicate such a thing, or at least make it palatable to her husband. Cressida had not the vocabulary, much less the knowledge, to say what she needed to.

Here, protected in her own bed, which Justin had visited but once in ten months, she tried to comfort herself with the knowledge that in a short time, all would be well between her and her adored husband. For so many years, she'd been granted every material luxury she could have wished for. The soft, featherdown mattress was a comfort she'd not enjoyed as the daughter of an impecunious parson, the luxurious bed linen something else she'd never taken for granted. No, she'd taken nothing for granted in her wonderfully happy marriage, not even Justin's love. But it was Justin's love and companionship she lacked now. It's what she missed more than anything, and she'd trade every physical luxury just to feel their hearts in tune once again; though Catherine often insinuated that after eight years of marriage it was not only expected, but inevitable, that a husband would stray.

A familiar step sounded just outside her room. With a start of horror, Cressida jerked upright, drawing the counterpane up to her neck as the door opened slowly, faint light spilling in from the corridor.

What was this? She'd said she'd meet him in a week? Had he misconstrued her invitation for an earlier assignation?

The words she might have used—should have used—died in her throat while her brain reeled in horror and her body felt closed-up and dried-up, not the life-pulsing vessel that had so desired the feel of her husband's body pressed against her—inside her—earlier.

"Good evening, my love," Justin whispered, carefully placing the candle on the dressing table as he lowered himself onto the edge of the bed. A golden glow suffused his face, the warmth of his expression kindling the need in Cressida's soul, if not her body. "You weren't asleep, I hope?" He leaned over her and tenderly began to stroke her shoulder.

Cressida forced herself to relax, lying back upon the bed as she smiled tremulously at him in the flickering light. "No, darling, I wasn't asleep." Her throat was so dry it hurt as she struggled with the urge to tell him of the confusing tumult of emotions that held her hostage. Emotions she could not explain or even justify. She wanted him, but she didn't. It made no sense.

Of course he'd come to visit her on account of the charade she'd shamelessly engineered. She should have expected nothing less.

Except that she was unprepared.

Completely.

His smile in the soft glow of light held a tender poignancy that tugged at her heartstrings. He was lonely. Just like she was, and now was the time to bare her soul. She could let him down gently, explain that in a week's time, when the woman at Mrs. Plumb's had told her what she wanted—needed—to know, she'd feel ready for an encounter like this. Justin was a kind and understanding man. A patient husband. He'd waited this long. He could certainly wait another week.

Horrified, she checked herself. It wasn't that simple, for her reluctance went deeper than simply denying Justin pleasure. She was his wife, the bearer of his children. His sons. How could she speak about *desire* when what she really wanted was knowledge of the methods that would prevent her conceiving the second son Justin deserved, desired and, yes, as his mother so frequently reminded her, *required?*

Her breath hitched in her throat while her mind raced over the best way to navigate these turbulent waters.

But every thought returned to the truth—she was disloyal and depraved. How could she refuse her husband his rights? To her body? To another son? Why would she want to when she was blessed above all women?

It had been months since Justin had visited her, an eternity since his gaze had raked her with that almost forgotten look of aching want that, in the bedroom, replaced the habitual affection he showed her during the day.

In the flickering candlelight ,the warmth of his smile gained heat as he rose to untie the cord of his banyan. It slid off his shoulders while he focused his gaze with unmistakable longing on her breasts, still confined in her lace-edged night shift. Cressida felt her palms begin to sweat, her breath fizzling in her throat as she feasted her eyes on the length of him.

Oh, he'd never reveal himself to her naked, but as she recalled the bronzed warrior she'd seen earlier that evening in the mist-filled chamber of brazenness, she knew Justin would look every bit as magnificent.

His good nature was etched in the fine lines around his usually warm brown eyes, now black with desire as they bore into her. His strong jaw was tense with intent, the well-sculpted cheek muscles sharp planes and shadows. Fashionably thick and curling hair brushed forward made him a handsome man. During the day, he was the urbane lord of the manor. Tonight, the finer civilities were stripped away as he pulled back the covers of the bed, the rapid rise and fall of his chest, his piercing stare and the exuberance of his manhood outlined by his nightshirt boldly declaring his rampant want.

For the first time, Cressida focused her attention upon the masculine *contours* of his fine linen shift. No, Justin would never come naked to her, and she'd never thought to explore the idea of skin to skin contact. Why? Because clearly skin to skin contact was not part of the marital act between a man and woman of Cressida's respective stations.

At least two layers of fabric were always trapped at some point between them.

Tonight's strange, wicked and depraved voyeurism had added a new perspective to her understanding of physical relations between men and women. It had shocked her yet excited her, filling her with longings she could not put into words.

Longings that stirred in her womb and made her damp, no, slick with desire. She ached to hold her husband to her breast, to wrap her legs around his waist and to rock with him in an embrace that would envelop them in sensation and sweep before it all the pain and loneliness of these ten long months.

But she could not.

Not yet.

Reason told her she need simply explain to Justin that she wasn't ready, yet reassure him that she soon would be.

Instead, panic ripped through her as the mattress dipped beneath Justin's weight; and reason—and with it, words—deserted her. What should she do? How could she explain that the only thing between her and Justin was 'a little matter' she'd attend to by next week? She'd already used her monthly excuses last week.

Her mind raced. She could hardly breathe through the fear as he slipped beneath the sheets and drew her to him, his fingers gently tugging at the ribbon of her night rail. She felt herself go rigid in his arms and nearly wept at the pain she'd soon cause him.

Taking her gasp as encouragement, and her rigidity as anticipation and perhaps a little fear after so long, he gently kissed her lips.

"Lovely creature," he whispered as the fabric yielded and her breasts spilled out into his hands.

Glancing up at his face, she was not surprised at the warmth of his love, radiating from him. Justin had always made her feel loved. As if she were a temple to the depth of his feelings for her, which ran so deep.

She whimpered as he found just the right pressure to knead her into compliance. His tongue, hot and wet, circled her nipple while one hand gently massaged her heated inner thighs and her body all but surrendered on the spot at the rightness of enslaving itself once more to him.

But she held herself back. She had to, even though the throbbing at the apex of her legs was agonizing. Once he recognized her need, she was doomed. She would conceive another child tonight, she knew it.

And another child, she truly believed, would kill her.

"My sweet Cressida, I have missed you." There was so much yearning in those few words before he transferred his attention to her other breast, she nearly wept. Meanwhile, she was acutely aware of the desperate need within her own body whipped up by his hot breath and skillful tongue.

Prickles of sensation skittered from the tips of her toes into the core of her belly, and she whimpered as she felt another rush of heat to her groin.

Justin found the hem of her night rail and gently tugged. Making the most of drawing it languidly up over her thighs, his fingers trailed a devastating path of lust and longing.

Feelings Cressida knew only too well. Feelings that would be the end of her.

Fighting every fiber of her needy body, she caged his hand against her thigh, halting its progress. Abruptly, he stopped, raising his head to look at her. In the pale glow, she saw the confusion that crossed his features. She'd met him part way, but now she was telling him she did not want him? She knew it was what he was thinking, and she forced out a thread of sound to tell him she loved and desired him as she always had.

"I'm sorry, Justin, I can't—" she croaked, her parched lips desperate for his understanding kiss.

But tonight Justin did not look as understanding as usual. He stilled, his hands withdrawing themselves from her body as he withdrew, the few inches between their heated flanks like a chasm of ice and fire.

"You don't want this?" A myriad of emotions flashed across his countenance—surprise, confusion, a brief flash of anger, then...

Nothing but dull resignation, oh, so much worse than anger and disappointment. Those she could meet with her own protests, perhaps propelling all that stood between them into the open. He might hate her for her disloyalty, but at least he'd understand.

Right now, even Cressida didn't understand. She had no idea of the nature of the practicalities that Miss Mariah had suggested might be the answer to her troubles. How could she properly explain to Justin her encounter with a common doxy who'd promised to show her ways to minimize conception during love-making? Or of the alternative sensory exploration she'd witnessed earlier in the evening? She could no more do that than sail into White's and join her husband for a whiskey at his club.

And then, as her gaze inadvertently beheld the size of his erection beneath his nightshirt, that alternative sensory exploration returned as a possible salvation.

She blocked her mind to the fact he might question her motivations when it was so out of character for her to take such an initiative. All she needed right now were delaying tactics, and if they made Justin happy, all the better.

Quickly, without saying a word, she pressed him onto his back and shimmied beneath the bedcovers, taking his erection in her hands and flicking her tongue across the tip of his manhood.

She heard his sudden intake of breath in the silence and stilled. Waiting. The man at Mrs. Plumb's had certainly enjoyed such a sensation, but what would Justin think when it was his wife attending to him in such a manner? Would he be similarly enthralled...or horrified?

At least it was better than any other alternative that involved procreation.

His entire body was rigid with surprise—and anticipation?—but he said nothing, just placed his hand gently on her head and breathed out in one long sigh.

Emboldened, Cressida drew the length of him into her mouth. How hard and hot it was. And how delightful it was to be the giver of such pleasure. Always she'd waited for Justin to initiate any variation on their bedroom delights.

Another groan. Surely she wasn't hurting him? The look of ecstasy on the face of tonight's bronzed warrior suggested a man did not find such attention painful. No, Justin's groan was definitely pleasure, for he was as tense as an arrow's bow. She shifted onto her knees, feeling the moisture between her thighs, a sign of her own excitement. She gently increased the pressure with her hands around his rigid shaft while her mouth moved up and down, her tongue flicking the length of him. She was balancing the score and she was enjoying doing it. She could do this every night without ever having to worry about conceiving again.

On this happy thought, she focused her entire attention upon pleasuring Justin, using her tongue along the length of his shaft—just as she'd seen it done at Mrs. Plumb's—circling it before taking him deeply into her mouth in a series of languorous thrusts.

"Cressida...darling..." His voice was hoarse as he dug his fingers into her shoulders. He seemed to be straining, using every ounce of willpower to keep still. She sensed what he must be feeling. She'd felt it many times, herself, when Justin's pleasuring had brought her to the cusp and she'd held back, feeling a strange mixture of both terror and ecstasy before spiraling into the glorious abyss.

She wanted Justin to feel the same wonderful sensations to which he'd introduced her. Exultation, pride and satisfaction welled up inside her. Without Mrs. Plumb's help, Cressida had discovered the secret to bringing her husband pleasure without implicating herself in anything that would return to haunt her.

Like another baby.

His breath was quick and shallow. The sound made her feel all-powerful. Her nipples ached and her sex pulsed in response, but she tried to close her mind to her own bodily sensations. They could most definitely not be acted upon.

"My glorious...darling...wife," he whispered, gripping her shoulders, and all the pent-up tension and fear Cressida had felt during these last months at the thought of intimacy with Justin simply drained away.

Until, with a gasp, he gently pushed aside her head, deftly drew her up beside him, rolled her onto her back and covered the length of her with his hard, needy body. She closed her eyes as she felt his erection press into her stomach before he adjusted himself lower.

Lower, so that his manhood was near her slick, wanting entrance and she was balanced on the edge of well-trained silence, contemplating the destruction of all her well-laid plans.

Being plundered by her husband was so very far from them, yet this was Justin, wanting her, needing her. Even as he slid into her, she felt her heart cry out at the rightness of this physical coupling, yet her brain roared its terrified objection.

One more week.

That's all she wanted. One more week so she could learn how a man could come inside a woman without making her pregnant. It was possible. Having learned this for fact, she knew she couldn't become a tacit collaborator in her own destruction, however much she wanted it at this moment.

Dragging her mouth from his, she struggled beneath him, pushing him away and wriggling her hips in clear objection rather than escalation of the sexual act.

"No!"

Her cry sounded much too harsh and her breathing, fast and clearly distressed, reverberated through the room.

Instantly he released her and she rolled onto her side. "Cressida?" His voice was thick with concern. "What is it?"

What is it?

What could she say? What *should* she say? *I don't want your child, Justin, and am busy investigating ways to ensure I need never become pregnant again, if you'll just be patient another week.*

If they were having this conversation before becoming intimate, she might have fumbled her way into making some semblance of sense. Right now, however, with fear and terror and guilt bombarding her with equal relentlessness, she did not know what to say.

"I'm so sorry, Justin," she whispered, withdrawing from his embrace and putting her hands to her temples as she swung her legs over the side of the bed, "but I feel another megrim coming on."

He dropped his hands, the faintest of exhalations stirring the hair at her temples, and Cressida felt his withdrawal, both physical and emotional, as he slowly got out of bed.

"You should have said something before, darling." He rose up before her, his look puzzled, but suspicious.

At the irony in his tone, she nearly abandoned her resolve not to hurl herself right back into his arms.

Nearly.

Only the fear of a fate equal to death in nine months stopped her.

CHAPTER 8

"You seem distracted, Justin. Bad news?"

Justin glanced up from the little writing desk in the corner of Mariah's sitting room at which he'd been working for the past hour, reconciling, yet again, the list of orphans who'd been delivered to and removed from Sedleywich eighteen years ago.

"I wish I could offer you concrete answers, but we have to be patient, Mariah," he muttered, though it was not his apparent preoccupation with the task with which Mariah had charged him that accounted for his distraction.

Cressida. Her behavior defied logic. Last night it was as if she'd enticed him to her merely so she could repulse him at the final juncture when that was not at all her nature. He closed his eyes and shivered with remembered longing as he recalled the brief feeling of being wanted once more by his wife.

Brief. He nearly snarled his bitterness. *Where* had she learned such a thing? That extraordinary moment when she'd shimmied down in the bed and indulged in an act no respectable woman would even *know* about?

He didn't want to answer that question. After all, he'd found her at a House of Assignation, for God's sake.

And why would she start on an act so calculated to whip up his desires only to reject him at the end?

He was confused and hurt. Suspicious, too. No, not suspicious that she'd actually betrayed him. He couldn't believe that of her. Not his angel; his innocent, big-hearted, *sweet* wife.

Yet what could have been the inspiration for such extraordinary bedroom antics? Antics that *she* had boldly initiated.

Only to reject him. That's what it all came down to.

For the first time since he could remember, Cressida had not been at breakfast this morning. Though he'd endured a hellish night, he'd forced himself to take his seat at the usual time, hoping to glean *something* over their habitual haddock and toast, even if no actual allusion were made to the previous evening's several extraordinary encounters.

But he couldn't dwell on that when there were other matters to attend to and he had a job to do.

Mariah came to stand beside him, bending to look over his shoulder. Her still lovely face bore a pallor and tightness that hinted at her stress, and Justin reached up to squeeze her hand.

"I agree with you, Mariah, that the most likely candidate is this Miss Madeleine Hardwicke, Lord Slitherton's betrothed. As you know, I am Patron of Sedleywich, and Miss Harwicke's sister-in-law, Annabelle Luscombe, is on the committee."

"Which makes muddying the trail all the easier." Mariah sighed. "Miss Hardwicke looks just as I did as a young girl, Justin, with her blue-black hair and Castilian features, yet she has Robert's strong nose." She twisted her hands. "Surely you can trace her origins and reveal the deception? I'm going insane, unable to think of anything but the growing suspicion my beloved Robert's evil mother retrieved our child from the Sedleywich Home for Orphans and somehow engineered that she be brought up as the child of *Robert's* sister." She covered her face with her hands and turned away, her words muffled as she continued, "Lord knows I was in no position to keep the child, I know that, but I was used, deceived, abandoned. Where was Robert when I needed him? We were so in love."

Justin reached for her hand and squeezed her fingers tight. When he saw the tears running silently down her cheeks, echoing the sadness and confusion in his own breast he was not able to speak of, he got to his feet and put his arms around his old friend. "Hush, Mariah, you are overwrought," he murmured as she clung to him and her body convulsed. "Do not blame Robert. You think men are all-powerful creatures? They are equally at the mercy of women when the balance is not in their favor." A frisson of despair speared him at the thought of Cressida and the power she wielded over him. "Love is a wonderful thing when two people are of one mind *and* that love is sanctioned by those around them who wield the power. Remember that Robert was not yet of age. He could do nothing in the face of his mother's opposition."

Mariah drew back, sniffing and attempting to smile, then she resumed her seat on the sofa while Justin returned to his desk. "You are a sensible man, Justin. Of course, I know what you say is true."

He drummed his fingers upon the document. "But I have to tell you that another possibility has presented itself." His smile failed to banish the rawness of her feelings. He knew desperate hope hovered beneath the surface of her restraint.

Wearily, she said, "Who is she, Justin?"

He shook his head. "It would be unfair to divulge names until her identity is confirmed."

Mariah rose and trailed to the window.

"If you have narrowed down the list to two, and indeed you know Miss Hardwicke's family, tell me if your investigations have concluded this at least..." She closed her eyes and the whitening of her knuckles, which matched the pallor of her face, tugged at Justin's heartstrings. "Will she want to know me?"

Justin pondered the question. Although he was navigating

these dangerous emotional waters as best he could, he felt close to being overwhelmed.

He shuffled the papers, wishing he'd been able to confide in Cressida from the start and cursing his promise to Mariah that he not breathe a word of her affairs to his wife. Cressida's wise counsel would have helped ensure he was dealing with the matter as sensitively as possible.

God, he certainly needed a lesson in that!

His overtures to Cressida last night only proved how utterly lacking in sensitivity he was. He'd completely misread the signals she'd sent him.

Impatiently, he pushed aside the document, desperate suddenly to leave Mariah's sitting room. He needed to return home so he could confront Cressida and learn why she ran hot and cold with him these days.

Most of all, he had to understand why she had followed him to Mrs. Plumb's and enticed him so overtly only to reject him later.

"It is never possible to predict a person's desire to know another," he said, hoping to do justice to Mariah's question while his thoughts remained with his wife. "This other young woman whose identity I discovered yesterday was removed from the orphanage the same day, and it is possible the two names were confused. I can tell you this, however—she lives in desperate poverty with a family named Potter, and your patronage would be gratefully received, I'm sure." He hesitated, then pressed on, his voice tinged with doubt. "However, the initial subject of my inquiries—"

"You mean Madeleine Hardwicke? Please suspend the lawyer speak, Justin."

Mariah's voice was bleak as she moved to stand before Justin, forcing him to look her in the eye. "If it *is* Madeleine Hardwicke, *she* won't want to know me..." she drew out the pause, adding quietly, "will she?"

Taking Justin's lack of response as confirmation for her worst fears, Mariah whispered, "Then my daughter is as lost to me as she ever was."

She turned away, saying brokenly, "I know I am being selfish and unreasonable. Would I wish her to have spent *her* life in poverty? Of course not. But what can I offer...someone like that... in my current position, when I was so hoping my suspicion to be entirely off the mark and that you would discover a young woman to whom I could be of some small use?"

Insensible to his soothing answer, her agitation increased as she paced. "I just cannot believe it of Robert's family. They wanted nothing to do with me. Robert, himself, abandoned me! Now this! Surely the risk would be too great if the truth were discovered?"

Justin tapped the desk with his fingers, mulling over everything he had learned during the past weeks. He'd spent hours studying the Sedleywich orphans register and following the complex chain of events that had obscured the origins of the child later presented to the world as the legitimate daughter of one of London's leading families. The daughter Mariah believed was her own.

"It's all in my report, Mariah," he said, indicating the document on the desk. "Soon, I shall receive information which will confirm, I suspect, that this second girl has no relevance to my investigation. As I've told you, Miss Hardwicke's family has gone to great lengths, and expense, to guard against any possibility of discovery, making my task so difficult. The only thing they could not take into account was family resemblance and a mother's need to know."

Mariah appeared not to have heard him. Only the rise and fall of her bosom revealed her feelings as she stared through the window into the street. "After all these years to finally discover my child..." Her voice trailed away before she added bitterly, "A child I can never claim!"

Her pain sliced at him, but he had nothing to offer except platitudes. She spoke the truth.

Mariah gave a wry laugh as she turned to say over her shoulder, "Only yesterday I told a young woman I was childless. Indeed, it is the truth, for I have never known my daughter and, now, it appears, I never will." Dropping her eyes, she added, "In a twist of irony, this poor young woman's anguish was caused by her ever-growing brood. Four, she said she'd had, in eight years, and suffering torments because she believed another would kill her."

Justin watched her push her dark hair back from her high forehead and wondered when it had become so tinged with gray. Just as he'd been struck by her handsome Castilian features when he'd first met her, he'd been struck by the continued rich gloss of her hair when she'd approached him three weeks before. Now it seemed dull and lifeless.

She was talking again, and he realized she was still referring to the young woman she'd met the previous day.

"I'd never have guessed it. She looked as innocent as a child, herself, beneath the thick veil and dressed all in black like an Italian widow. And frightened. This was no place for her. She admitted as much, but I think she'd have entered a tiger's den if she could have reclaimed her husband and poured out her heart to him."

Justin, who had been scanning his report once more while preparing to leave, looked up.

"She was here to *reclaim* her husband, did you say?"

Maria nodded, chewing her thumbnail as she continued to stare into the street. "If we women were only given rudimentary knowledge of the facts when it came to the realities of marriage, this poor woman would not be so desperate and I"—her shoulders slumped— "might still be happily married."

He could barely attend to her reflections and hoped his voice did not betray him. Trying to assimilate the multitude of questions jostling for precedence, he asked carefully, "How did you and this woman meet?"

"She was near fainting in the corridor, so great was her fear of discovery. She'd been told her husband was here, though she seemed to have scant notion as to what she would do when she found him."

"She ventured to this place, alone, to find her husband?" Justin balled his fists and forced himself to breathe evenly. Mariah could be describing no one else but his wife. "Because someone told her this is where she'd find him?"

"I think she just wanted to know if he was here. She said she was terrified of more children. Apparently, her mother died giving birth to her fifth."

"What!" Justin gave no thought to the force of his exclamation. *Afraid of more children?* Cressida doted on their offspring. Increasingly, she chose to spend her time with them, rather than her husband.

Mariah was speaking once more. He tried to concentrate on her words while the implications of her assertion filtered through to his brain. He'd begun to think his wife's earlier enthusiasm for the marriage act was purely for procreation, not recreation. That while she sought a cessation of marital relations with the nursery full, she'd also lost interest in the shared intimacy he still so greatly craved. Not once had she ever suggested he take precautions to protect against further pregnancies.

Shock was swept away by the most intense dismay as he acknowledged they'd never properly had the conversation. Such talk was lewd, sinful... Good Lord, he thought with a start, perhaps Cressida did not even know such prevention was possible. It was not a conversation one had with one's wife, though he had tried...

The realization of Cressida's real and terrible fears swamped him, and the words of his report, upon which his eyes were unconsciously trained, blurred. Uncurling his fingers, he raked his hand through his hair.

He straightened in his chair, breathing carefully as he acknowledged how gravely he had failed his innocent, lovely wife. It was his duty to comfort and protect Cressida, to make her happy. He was ten years older, with experience beyond anything she could ever know. Just as Cressida had no knowledge of sexual relations outside their own bedroom, she'd have no idea how to translate her fear into words. Lord almighty, she'd known nothing on her wedding night, and when her first pregnancy had been confirmed, she'd asked from where the baby would emerge!

Now, instead of broaching a topic that Justin suspected was not discussed even among women, she'd practiced the only thing she knew would protect against conception.

Abstinence.

Resistance.

A surge of protectiveness sent the blood roaring to his head and moisture stung his eyes. How long had his precious, darling Cressida been caught in this dark, terrible place, unable to translate her feelings for him into anything physical for fear of the consequences? Last night she had come so far, taken such bold, brave steps, faltering only at the last when he had failed, yet again, to understand her terrors.

The chair nearly toppled in Justin's sudden haste to return home and take Cressida in his arms and counter every fear of hers in the most loving, practical way of which he was capable.

"Apologies for my abrupt departure, Mariah," he said, "but I have just recalled an urgent appointment. Tomorrow I shall return with, I hope, confirmation to set both our minds at rest." In three quick strides he was at the door. In less than ten minutes, he'd be home. He'd thought Cressida was playing games with him. No, he'd had no idea what Cressida was doing, but now he knew the truth. Surely, if he acted quickly, he could rekindle their precious love before she had drifted too far from him?

"That's unlike you, Justin."

He could barely answer, for his thoughts were concentrated entirely on the task at hand. "Sounds like your poor new friend's husband is an ignorant boor," he muttered, his hand upon the doorknob, "who deserves to sleep alone."

Great was his disappointment to learn upon arriving in Bruton Street that Cressida had apparently responded to an urgent summons from her great-aunt Jane who lived in Bath and who claimed to be upon her deathbed. Brimble, the butler, said he was uncertain when Lady Lovett would return.

CHAPTER 9

Fumbling in her reticule for her handkerchief as she stood uncertainly in a dim passage at Mrs. Plumb's the following Wednesday, Cressida mopped her eyes. These tears! Where did they come from? Soon she would be confined to the asylum if she did not find a remedy for the nervous anxiety that afflicted her.

She'd spent the previous five days with her great-aunt before returning this afternoon to find Justin not at home. She had to admit she'd been rather relieved.

If only she could control this infernal shaking. Tonight... What might it bring? It all depended so much on whether Miss Mariah was telling her the truth or not. Could she really have a remedy for Cressida's woes? Was there really something so simple as a means of adequate protection each time she accepted her husband into her bed? Even something to lessen the risks was better than nothing. In all their years together, there'd been no talk of *that*, though she remembered broaching the difficult subject with Catherine after she'd discovered she was with child for the fourth time.

"My, my but you'll bankrupt poor Justin if you insist on producing a daughter for him every year," her cousin had said, pretending jocularity. "I've given James his two sons, which suits him very nicely."

Feeling overwhelmed, Cressida had struggled not to break down in tears as she asked, "Is there some secret I'm not aware of, Catherine, that you speak like that? Of course I want to give Justin a son. It's my duty. But you? You may well start producing daughters, too."

"Not likely," Catherine had answered wryly, and Cressida had longed to quiz her more. She had, in fact, obliquely charged Catherine with knowing of some practice to ensure that she didn't produce girls, but Catherine had simply patted Cressida's knee in that maddeningly superior way of hers and said as she always did, "Don't ask me, Cressy, ask Justin. You stopped confiding in me long ago when you learned that your darling husband was the font of all knowledge."

But of course Cressida could not ask Justin when she was growing bigger with the child they hoped would be the longed-for heir and which, when born, turned out to be their darling Emily. Cressida had sobbed with dismay at the time, though she'd loved Emily like the rest of their girls, and so had Justin. Ah, but then Thomas had finally arrived, and Cressida thought that finally she'd somehow find the words she needed now that Justin had his son.

Instead, she simply reverted back to the tongue-tied, country dormouse Catherine had teased since they were children, smiling and pliant on the outside, tormented by her ignorance on the inside.

"My dear girl!" Her friend greeted her warmly and led her into a small conservatory at the back of the house.

"It is such a lovely evening we can sit here, as my own sitting room is currently occupied." Miss Mariah patted the seat beside her on the cane sofa. "I'm glad you came...and dressed for action, too, I see," she added, referring to Cressida's revealing black evening gown. With its deep neckline and figure-hugging cut, it was very different to her widow's weeds of the previous week. "I promise you, a few minutes are all it will take for me to explain what would advance society's happiness and end so much suffering."

From the tray on the table beside them, she took two glasses of sherry and handed one to Cressida.

In the natural light, Miss Mariah looked different from the previous week. There was now no sign of the gray that had peppered her hair, her gown was of fine blue silk and her eyes sparkled. Cressida was surprised she felt no revulsion for this creature who traded her body for what she could not otherwise procure. Unlike Cousin Catherine, Cressida tried not to be so quick to judge others, yet the fact was that Cressida was about to take advice—perhaps the most important advice of her life—from a prostitute. Or, at least a retired one.

Miss Mariah leaned across the small space between them and asked with clear enthusiasm, "Now, where shall we begin? I do admire a young woman who sets out to help herself. You have been an inspiration to me, for I was a lusterless creature last week, I'll admit it." She raised her own glass. "You helped me see that, regardless of our trials, we must embrace the future."

Cressida took a nervous gulp of the amber-colored liquid and looked down at her gloved hand, clenched in her lap. "My husband —" she began, feeling a surge of longing for the man she'd hurt, neglected and lied to over the past week and whose arms she could not wait to feel around her. A week with her fractious aunt had heightened her desire for the simple comfort of his company.

"Your husband is a capital place to start. I've no idea what kind of man he is, but, as it is clear you are deeply in love with him, I cannot imagine he'd not be completely amenable to doing his part to lessen the risk of increasing your already large brood when it comes to lovemaking."

Heat seared Cressida's face and throat as she spluttered on her sherry.

Her friend laughed. "How many years did you say you'd been married? Eight? Nearly as long as myself. My dear, the way we entertain our husbands is at the very core of how they regard us, and if you are too afraid even to mention what is at the root of your fear then I see you have a very great problem indeed."

Cressida forced down her embarrassment. If this woman spoke the truth, her world was about to begin anew. She'd grown up with a maiden aunt and cousin who'd taught her nothing about the business and a domineering mother-in-law who'd made it clear that a reluctant wife was undutiful and unnatural. A knowledgeable stranger was as good as anyone to dispense the kind of advice she needed right now.

She put down her empty glass and laced her fingers in her lap, the anticipation of what she hoped to hear making her heart race. "Miss Mariah, after I left you last week, I chanced upon my husband unexpectedly in this house," she said, quietly. "Yes, I was shocked, but we were both in masquerade," she continued, going on to explain what had transpired, though her voice broke as she described the hurt and confusion on Justin's face when she'd told him she had a megrim.

"A megrim? Good Lord, my dear girl, how have you managed this past week if your husband was so full of expectation upon meeting you last Wednesday?"

Cressida's mouth trembled. "I...haven't," she confessed. "I was a coward, I know. Instead of confiding in him, I went to my great-aunt's, for I couldn't face him. I didn't know what to do." She raised tear-filled eyes toward Miss Mariah, her self-disgust weighing down on her as much now as it had a week ago. Poor Justin. She hadn't seen him since that night. What must he think?

"Oh, my dear, what a terrible time you've had of it." Miss Mariah leaned forward and patted Cressida's knee, and Cressida felt the genuine concern that was so lacking when Catherine did the same. "If I'd known this would happen, I'd have got down to business straightaway. As it is, we've not a moment to lose. Let me assure you, you're not the first who's sought my advice. Mrs. Plumb's salon attracts so many like you, women and men with hearts full of love but living in circumstances whereby acting on that love is tantamount to a death sentence."

Cressida covered her hands. "A child born to an unmarried woman would be like a death sentence, though it is a mortal sin and should be justly punished, I suppose," she whispered. "But I am a married woman, and my only duty is to provide my husband with a son and to manage as best I can. What I am doing—or wish to do—is a sin."

"Nonsense!"

Cressida blinked at Miss Mariah's robust tone.

"Perhaps it is in the eyes of the church and some members of society but that it their problem." The older woman spoke with extraordinary confidence and disregard for conventional wisdom. "It's true that knowledge of methods to avoid conception is sought by many of the unmarried women who frequent Mrs. Plumb's Salon. For some, trading on their natural charms is their only choice unless they are to starve."

"There is always a choice. Selling one's body is...is abhorrent," Cressida whispered with a shiver. She'd overheard such sentiments discussed between Justin and Catherine's husband, James. In fact, she still blushed to have come silently upon such a conversation when on a warm summer's evening she'd gone into the garden in search of Justin and heard her husband speak these very words to James, "Taking one's pleasure outside marriage is abhorrent and a mortal sin."

It had been so shocking to hear the strength he'd injected into his declaration, not to mention such an odd thing for Justin to say to Catherine's husband, whom Cressida had to admit she had never liked. He was distant and uncommunicative, and he barely ever looked at Catherine when he spoke to his wife, though Catherine was always gushing about his latest achievements and, more often, his gilded prospects.

Cressida had been confused by James' response, "What if it's the only pleasure on offer? By God, Justin, it's a bit rich to preach from your rarefied position."

Cressida had quickly left them to hurry back to the house, uncomfortable at having heard what she clearly should not have.

Nevertheless, Justin's disgust for such conduct echoed the strictures with which she'd been brought up. The only good woman was a virtuous woman, otherwise she was condemned both on earth and in the afterlife.

"Surely they know they'll go to hell?" she added, confused and embarrassed when she saw the way Miss Mariah looked at her.

Miss Mariah sighed and began in measured tones, "Suppose, if you will, you were a parson's daughter—"

Cressida pressed her lips together and shifted uncomfortably. Surely this woman knew nothing of her origins? But Miss Mariah was talking again.

"And suppose you have every expectation of making a fine match because the squire's son asks you to stand up with him at two dances every assembly you attend over the course of several months." Miss Mariah shook her head. Clearly she was recounting the tale of someone she knew. "But then one day you were out riding and came off your horse, and who should come by but the handsome squire's son, who gallantly puts you into his carriage"— Miss Mariah paused meaningfully—"and then drives you all the way to London, where he ruins you. Deprived now of your virtue, what choice has a young woman but to become this man's mistress? For, as you know, his influence in his local area will trump the tale of the impecunious parson's daughter who was known to have set her sights on the best catch of the county."

"You're talking about Minna, aren't you?" Cressida asked quietly.

"Indeed, I am. Before she became one of the vestal virgins, she was no different from you, I'll wager, except that fate played her a shocking hand. Now she's here, earning what little she can by dancing in shifts that leave little to the imagination now that her seducer has tired of her. For many months she has been adamant she will not sell her body, though she is all but starving. But now her high ideals are in jeopardy if she is merely to survive and she has asked me—"

"Minna has consulted *you* about such things, too?" Cressida knew she should not want to know the details, and yet Miss Mariah had struck a chord. Minna's upbringing was so similar to hers except that the young man who had courted Cressida had been her darling, loyal and honorable Justin, who had almost immediately offered marriage.

Miss Mariah nodded. "She has, yes."

"She should stand firm," Cressida burst out. "If she's survived these many months then surely she will find one man who will offer her...marriage. And he'd only do that if he knew she was...virtuous."

Miss Mariah raised one eyebrow. "Life is not always so black and white, my dear. Recently, poor Minna received news that her father has died, plunging the family into poverty. Now her sister will be forced to marry an abhorrent creature who has offered for her ad whom she will be forced to wed, for the family has no money now and she has no dowry."

Cressida had heard of many such stories. "Women are forced to wed against their hearts' wishes all the time. I'm sorry for it, and I'm the first to concede how lucky I am, but—"

"Is it wrong for a woman who is already ruined and believes she's destined for hell to want to save her virtuous and innocent young sister from a life of unhappiness?"

Cressida frowned. "No," she said dubiously, wondering on what basis Miss Mariah's argument could be furthered. Slowly, she added as understanding dawned, "But if I were Minna's unmarried sister, I'd rather die than know she'd sold her body to help me."

"It's not that simple, my dear." Miss Mariah smiled sadly. "Indeed, it never is. You see, Minna has been made a handsome offer by a stranger who wishes for just five nights in her bed. It is an extraordinary offer, for it is generous enough to provide Minna with the means of offering her sister an avenue out of a lifetime of marital unhappiness and servitude. Yes, Minna feels it is abhorrent to sell her body...and yet what sacrifice would she not make to ensure her young sister does not endure the pain of being thrust into the hands of an uncaring man with whom she'll have to live for the rest of her life?"

Cressida's shoulders slumped. It was all so confusing, and the more she heard of such tales, the more her own moral code shifted on its axis. Nothing was straightforward, it seemed. "What is Minna going to do?" Of course it was nothing to do with her, but the pretty, fair-haired girl could have been any of the debutantes she'd grown up with and who'd gone on to make respectable marriages.

"She is considering accepting this offer, as I said. This man has not revealed himself, so that makes her decision difficult, but increasingly she seems to place less importance on her own life, which is ruined and unhappy, and more on securing her sister's happiness through her own sacrifice." Miss Mariah sent Cressida a warning look. "Nevertheless, Minna will not risk bringing an innocent child into the world to bear the shame of illegitimacy and to be forced into a life of slavery to men, so that's why she's consulted me on the many ways to prevent or limit the risk of conception, and indeed ways to prevent a pregnancy from proceeding."

Cressida gasped. "From proceeding? Why, that's murder!"

"Is it murder to drink the tea made from a common herb? Would you call a poor woman who has twelve children, no money and a drunken husband a murderer for drinking pennyroyal tea to regulate her courses?"

Cressida shrugged, unsure how to answer. All her ideas on morality had been founded using very different examples to support them.

Miss Mariah's expression softened. "But I can help you *before* you need to resort to such drastic measures, for it *is* possible for you to enjoy marital relations without constantly fearing you'll beget a child."

All thoughts of poor Minna's desperate plight receded as Cressida leaned forward, the urge to learn filling her with hope. She wanted to know everything Justin knew. Knowledge was power. Cressida could use it to conduct her life and use her body as she wished. She didn't have to be like the women Miss Mariah described. Theirs was another world and their reasons for wanting to avoid conception very different from hers, though they all had one thing in common—the need to be in control of their bodies and fertility.

The thought was radical. What woman did she know who thought that way? There must be something wicked and wrong with her, and yet was this the secret nobody was prepared to discuss in public?

How had Catherine succeeded in giving birth to two sons only in a marriage of similar length to Cressida's? Did she already know what Miss Mariah was about to teach Cressida?

Or had she simply denied James since the second boy was in the cradle?

Fascinated, Cressida watched Miss Mariah reach into a crimson velvet drawstring bag. Upon the inlaid table in front of them, she laid out a small sponge and a brown bottle labeled vinegar together with a small, brown paper bag. Beside this she placed a strange, oblong object made of, if Cressida didn't know better, some animal membrane.

"Men have been using French letters for centuries, but we women have our little secrets, too. Now, my dear, I am going to give you the kind of advice and information I'd have given my own daughter," her voice hitched, "had I been able."

Cressida didn't miss the lapse of composure. She sympathized. A woman's chief purpose was to beget and rear her children. Wasn't she blessed to have had four, and all so robust, for at last Thomas appeared to be growing out of his childish maladies. This last week, for the first time, he'd run about Great-Aunt Jane's country garden like a little colt. How she wished Justin could have seen it. She shook her head quickly to banish the thought and returned to the here and now. Poor Miss Mariah had had to forgo the joy of a family in order to support herself through the pleasures of the flesh, making money in perhaps the only way she was able.

The sheath of sheep's gut—for that's what Miss Mariah now said it was—hung limply from her fingers. "Of all methods, the French letter is the most effective means of preventing conception, though not all women can persuade their husbands or lovers of the need to use them, meaning of course they must have alternative methods at their disposal."

Cressida's cheeks burned, and she nearly choked on her horror as Miss Mariah began to caress the object, half smiling. "Some women, however, are able to induce their men to don the French letter by turning the process of easing it over their manly organ when excitement builds into a sensual game. If you wish for a demonstration, there are those in this salon—"

"No!" Cressida squeaked. "Just...explain it to me." Had she really gone so far even as to ask *that*? For an explanation? She'd never heard of such a thing, yet now she looked at it more closely she could see how it must work.

"The seed which would otherwise be spilled inside the woman, who then may go on to conceive, is contained within the French letter, which can be washed ready for future use." Miss Mariah handed it to Cressida. "Feel it. Get used to it. Indeed, take it. It may be all you need to save you another twenty years of doubt and anguish if not the pain and danger of multiple pregnancies."

Cressida took it reluctantly. "I could never ask my husband to use such a thing," she whispered, "however much I may wish it. Please don't look so disappointed, it's just that in my position I could never explain where I came by such knowledge."

"Then you must induce *him* to come by the knowledge himself, and to encourage the pursuit of such knowledge. It's up to you to convey to him your desire to limit your nursery so that he can take responsibility for his role in ensuring he doesn't foist a child upon you every year." Miss Mariah reached for the bottle of vinegar. "For centuries, women have understood that douches such as vinegar or lemon juice following the sexual act are beneficial for minimizing the risk of pregnancy, though of course it is the man who chooses *coitus interruptus* or to wear a French letter, who is most beloved of women who wish for the pleasures rather than the consequences of bedroom play." She cocked an eyebrow. "I gather you fall into the category of wives who do at least enjoy the pleasures of the bedroom."

Cressida nodded, for the first time able to look Miss Mariah in the eye. Everything the woman said was common sense, so why should Cressida act like a shrinking violent when she was here to gain the strength she needed to be the wife and bedfellow her husband desired?

"And now we come to the seeds of the Queen Anne's Lace plant, another useful weapon in your armament." Miss Mariah picked up the paper bag and reached for Cressida's hand, turning up the palm and pouring some grains onto it.

"These seeds, when taken some days before, or even for some days immediately after the act, have proven enormously beneficial for many women seeking to prevent conception."

Cressida stared at them. How tiny and harmless they looked. Unlike a bottle of vinegar in her dressing room and a hasty exit to douche herself, which would alert Justin's curiosity if not concern, she might easily swallow a handful of these seeds.

"Where can I get these?" she asked, aware of the excitement in her voice.

"I have a dear friend who is proficient in the herbal medicines, and she supplies me from time to time. You can take these now." A warning note crept into Miss Mariah's voice. "However, I would prefer that you discussed your fears with your husband before you secretly went about finding ways to limit your family. Indeed, this is a discussion for the two of you, otherwise grave misunderstandings could arise." Her expression clouded. "I know that more than anyone."

Despite the lecture and the dampening knowledge that she must indeed speak to Justin, Cressida was almost bursting with the excitement of so many possibilities within her grasp. If what Miss Mariah was telling her was true, Cressida could look forward to enjoying long, loving sessions with Justin and loving a smaller family than otherwise might be the case.

Tending to Great-Aunt Jane had been a trial. While Cressida had nursed her fractious relative, she'd also nursed her own confusion, her lackluster spirits bolstered by the daily, loving letters her husband had sent her. Wonderful Justin deserved far better than simple, fearful Cressida. However, as Cressida had wrinkled her nose at the foul-smelling ointment she'd used to rub her ungrateful great-aunt's arthritic legs, she'd also found herself blushing as she'd channeled her mental energies into concocting a thrilling scenario that would set Justin's senses on fire. Thanks to the now dreamlike experience of Mrs. Plumb's back chamber and Miss Mariah's instruction on lovemaking without consequences, Cressida's marriage, she now felt with increasing conviction, was about to take off in a whole new, thrilling direction.

CHAPTER 10

Justin couldn't remember when he'd been at such pains to ensure his turnout was immaculate. Finally, Wednesday evening had come around again, signaling a week since the dreadful confusion with Cressida in Mrs. Plumb's sitting room, and here he was, about to return to his friend's modestly furnished drawing room, making another attempt at getting his necktie just right.

After Cressida's abrupt departure last week for Bath, he'd been at a loss. A complete and utter loss. For the first four days, their communication had consisted of one brittle letter informing him of her health—a poor response to the reams of loving good wishes *he'd* poured onto the page. Then, extraordinarily, yesterday, after a long description of the children's activities, she'd written that she'd missed him and that she looked forward to meeting him...

He took another breath to calm himself as he reflected on those uncharacteristic words, so full of promise.

"...perhaps in unexpected circumstances tomorrow evening, when all shall be revealed."

All shall be revealed? Images of her literal disrobing competed with a frank explanation of her torments. Justin was fully prepared to offer a very loving reception in both instances.

Then, out of the blue this afternoon, Mariah had mentioned seeing again the 'poor woman with so many children', obliquely alluding to the 'instruction' she'd offered and which she hoped would benefit her.

Was Cressida really returning this evening, armed with new knowledge, to finish what they'd started the week before? On the one hand, he felt deeply remiss and neglectful that she'd had to resort to a stranger like Mariah for instruction—on exactly *what*, he could only imagine. But he had to let that go. What husband could speak to his gently reared wife in such terms unless she broached the subject with him? No, this was women's business.

And yet...

With a curse, he tossed aside the crumpled neck linen that had failed to meet his expectations of style. He'd dismissed his manservant for the night—tying his cravat was Justin's responsibility—but as he tried again with a fresh length of lawn, he wondered suddenly at *his* dependence. In a moment, he would recall Dowling, who with a deft flick of his wrist would whip Justin's rig-out into shape, and Justin would step out with every confidence of being up to the mark. Dowling had been in his employ since he'd set up in his own residence before he'd married. The older man had been an arbiter of style and a font of knowledge to the youthful Justin, who had been just finding his own feet in a world of opportunity.

But who had Cressida relied upon for advice and to bolster her confidence? Her mother had died when Cressida was just a child, and as a poor parson's daughter, she'd not had a lady's maid. The two females closest to her were her crotchety maiden aunt, who of course would know nothing with regard to what went on in the bedroom, and her dreadful cousin, Catherine.

Justin had been her only honest barometer when it came to gauging expectations within marriage. Cressida would have assumed Justin wanted sons—a backup for sickly Thomas—when he was more than happy with the family he had.

By the time Justin was satisfied at the way his coat sat and was at last at Mrs. Plumb's, hope that his wife was coming tonight had mutated into the most extraordinary maelstrom of emotions he'd ever experienced as he envisaged the variety of scenarios that might ensue once they were together again.

Still, he could not push aside the responsibility and guilt he felt at Cressida's apparent torment, and his attempts at communicating this on paper littered his study.

He'd not revealed to Mariah that Cressida was in fact the woman who had bared her heart to her. Mariah's initial criticism of his wife had stung. It might even be possible—though he doubted it—that Mariah was jealous of the wife who'd usurped her place in Justin's heart eight years ago.

In the intervening week, Justin had tried to focus his attention on Mariah's business and, to that end, at least, he'd been largely successful. Confirmation had been received discounting the second girl who might have been Mariah's daughter. Now his report was finished and his work for Mariah concluded.

At least that was one thing at which he'd succeeded for Lord knew, he was feeling utterly beastly with regard to his failures toward his wife.

Justin was just pouring himself a fortifying brandy when there was a tap at the door.

Mariah had promised him privacy in her small sitting room for the evening while he finished his report, saying she'd join him at about midnight, after she finished performing in the salon.

He tensed. Cressida? It was more than probable that the timid rapping was his wife, and yet his response put him in the league of some inexperienced greenhorn. His hand shook as he replaced the stopper of the cut-glass decanter.

Relief that she'd come surged while excitement roared through his veins. Could it really be her? He'd half expected she'd lose her nerve, but the fact that she had not was extraordinarily exciting. Intoxicating, in fact.

Commanding himself, he assumed the safest position—that of

languid host, kindly disposed to receive his invited guest. Such a relaxed attitude when the maid showed Cressida in would help calm her no doubt disordered nerves. And his. She might be his wife of eight years, but the tenuous resumption of physical relations was too serious a matter for him to risk frightening her at this early stage.

The door opened and he adjusted his mask, balled his fists and forced a smile, his breath leaving him in a rush. He felt his temperature rise and swallowed, his mouth suddenly dry.

The widow had returned.

But this was not the bereaved, frightened and needy creature who'd approached him in this room the week before.

Nor the graceful, demure goddess of his household and his wife of eight years.

No, this was a strange, alluring vixen-like creature with eyes that sparkled at him like gems through the slits of her demi-mask and deep pink lips that curved with lustful intent.

Cressida looked utterly magnificent in a stunning, figure-hugging sheath of midnight-shot silk encrusted with black beads, which twinkled when they caught the light. Her corn gold hair was threaded through with a thin rope of pearls, tendrils framing the lovely, oval-shaped face he knew so well but that was now obscured by her ornate opera mask.

Even through her disguise, he could see she was looking at him like he could imagine her looking at no man, not even her husband —indeed, with such lascivious intent that he felt his manhood leap to attention in such a desperate call for immediate satisfaction that he had to drag air into his lungs to stave off the reeling in his head.

Dear God, he'd never beheld such a captivating creature, and the fact that she was his wife and that clearly she wanted him brought him so much pleasure it took all his willpower not to close the few feet between them and ravish her on the spot.

Cressida's frank examination made it clear there was no need to extend the polite preliminaries. A small toss of her head and a knowing look was all it took to have him cross the floor in two great strides to greet her, turning the lock in the door behind her before crushing her in his arms. She wilted like a hothouse flower, pliant and clinging, and the light fragrance of lavender water that seemed then to epitomize her essence of goodness nearly undid him on the spot. If she did not want more children, he knew how to ensure the loving frolics he was so looking forward to could become a daily ritual without ever adding to their family.

The blend of ruse and ritual was a heady combination. How many times had he held Cressida in his arms as adoring husband, passionate lover and comforting helpmate? Never, however, had he done so while pretending both were strangers. It offered license to behave with playful artifice, and as he grazed her jawline with kisses, murmuring, "The lonely widow need not remain lonely," he was sure he sensed her tacit acceptance, that gone were the rules that had hitherto governed their relations.

God, he was mad to have let her drift away like he had, he reflected as he cupped her shapely bottom, pulling her tightly against him so she could be in no doubt as to his arousal. He would let her know what he wanted now, instead of risking confusion and flight once matters had proceeded.

Her warm, sweet breath tickled his ear as she clung to him. "I'd hoped you'd be waiting for me," she whispered, offering him greater access to her bosom so he could slip his hand inside her bodice and gently squeeze one taut—and, he hoped, aching —nipple.

In the dim light, the fire crackled and the heat level rose.

"Waiting for you, my love?" He rasped in a breath. "I've been waiting for nothing else." His hands were unable to halt their exploration of her shapely body as he trailed kisses over her décolletage and shoulders. Since Thomas' birth, she'd grown slender again. Yet it was not only her body that sent him wild. It was everything. He had to make sure she knew. "I've been insane with desire...driven mad the whole week at the mere thought of this."

Her shuddering sigh suggested she ached with the same need

that consumed him. He wondered how any woman could combine such sweet innocence with such a provocative manner. He felt doubly blessed. He was a man who could enjoy two wives—the demure angel of the house she presented to the world, and the lust-crazed vixen in the bedroom.

"My beautiful widow has the most magnificent breasts," he murmured, nibbling her lower lip, loving the way she arched against him, thrusting her chest against his in open invitation for more of his tender ministrations. He was pleased to find that the tiny buttons that fastened her gown ran down the front rather than the back. With his right hand still cupping her delectable bottom—she was not part of the daring set who'd adopted the craze of wearing underwear—his other deftly undid the top five pearl fastenings, his senses thrilling to hear her low groan as her breasts spilled out of their confinement, for tonight she was without her constricting stays. Beneath her figure-hugging gown was just flesh.

"I have missed my husband so very much," she gasped, whimpering as he suckled first one soft, white mound then the other. "So very much," she reaffirmed on a sigh, stroking his cheek while he rolled her nipple against the palm of his hand before tickling it with his tongue. He felt her tense, then her legs buckled as he gripped her hips, grinding them against his almost painful erection as he took possession of her lips once more.

So much for taking it gently. The pace escalated quickly, yet his response was entirely governed by her own eagerness. He would not hasten this and be caught out by his own urgency when he knew the importance of this first time after so long. Cressida needed to be reassured, though not in words, that she would have no fear of conceiving another child. The fact was that she'd followed him here, choosing to reignite their passion in its rooms away from their own house and their own servants. She'd clearly discovered Justin was innocent of seeking out its pleasures and was here for some other purpose, and now she, too, had daringly chosen to utilize its 'other' purpose.

Cressida's mouth, usually so sweetly yielding for the chaste kisses she'd always enjoyed, was a cavern of unexpected delights. She kissed him back with passion, her little tongue darting, licking, exploring. Her breath came in short, staccato bursts as he led her to the mantelpiece, only just able to restrain himself, and placed her hands on the shelf at shoulder height, facing her away from him so that he could nuzzle her neck, his hands roaming all over her. The grinding of her hips and her sighs of pleasure as he contoured her thighs and skimmed her waist before pulling her against him to suckle her earlobes left him in no doubt as to her enthusiasm.

Sinking to his knees, Justin gently turned her round, lifting the hem of her skirt to trail hot kisses from her ankles, up her calves to her knees. He felt her tense as he reached her inner thighs. She'd not been pleasured like this before, but then she'd been an innocent when he'd married her, and lovemaking was for producing heirs. Now that she'd obviously, and no doubt unexpectedly, learned a thing or two at Mrs. Plumb's, she'd come to him with the express purpose of indulging in lovemaking with absolutely no desire for procreation, and Justin was determined she'd enjoy it to the full.

She was his paragon of virtue, his vixen of pleasure. She was everything to him, and he longed to be reinstated to the exalted position she'd once held him in. He'd failed her once, but he'd not do so again.

Justin's explorations to the font of her desire were smooth, slippery and unimpeded. He could never remember feeling his wife quite so excited. Arching her back, Cressida tried to push him away as she moaned her guilty pleasure—clearly she'd not expected to be so enthralled by this new pastime he'd devised for her.

By the light thrown out by the Argand lamp, he could see the ecstasy in her half-closed eyes when, still kneeling, he tipped his head up to reassure himself that the book in which he'd placed the French letter was still on the mantelpiece. It was an observation that sent another spear of lust charging through him.

"Dear Lord, no!" she cried as he kissed her swollen bud. Her movements were becoming jerky, he could tell she was on the cusp of her pleasure, but long experience had taught him how to measure her responses, bringing her to the summit before letting her down again.

He was nearly ready to explode himself. It had been so long, though he thought he'd conditioned himself to a life of celibacy. Now he realized how combustible his responses to his sweet wife really were. She held his heart in the palm of her hand. But he would not let her down. Right now it was only her pleasure that was important, though her excitement merely ratcheted up his own. When she gripped a hank of his hair and did not let go as her pleasure mounted, her excitement traveled all the way down the shaft to spear his heart. Then farther, to his swollen, hard erection, and he had to remind himself once again that it was not his night to indulge in his own pleasure as heat swept through him and the hairs on the back of his neck stood up.

Carefully, he continued his honed assault upon her senses, dipping several fingers inside her as he swept his tongue across her most sensitive parts, loving the heat and scent of her excitement. Why had he not imagined indulging in such wicked pastimes with his own wife before? Cressida was in paradise and so was he.

She gasped, one minute begging him to stop, the next minute begging for more. He'd never seen her in such thrall, making his own excitement almost unbearable. It was a paradox to say he'd not indulge in his own pleasure, when her pleasure was his. He felt he was playing her like a finely tuned instrument, and his success in creating such responses was fascinating. He longed to tear the mask from her face and then discard his own mask, revealing themselves, but he sensed it was this distance from reality which enabled Cressida, for now, to hurl herself with such enthusiasm into their sexual congress.

Later she would accept him back into her bed with her former enthusiasm, now that all restraint had been banished between them and each knew, secretly, the desires of the other.

Her climax was cataclysmic. She bucked and moaned, twisting her hands in his hair as she fought against it, finally crumpling to the floor beside him, her breath coming in short bursts.

Kneeling, he stared at her, a slow grin spreading across his face. Clearly she was determined not to show herself, for the mask remained firmly in place, but she'd know that he'd know her body, her responses, the scent of her desire, anywhere. Justin had never believed in keeping secrets, but tonight was an exception. If secrecy for the meantime gave Cressida the confidence to realize her potential in the marital chamber, she could have as much of it as she wanted.

In a minute, he would retire to regain his composure now that he'd taken her to the zenith of her pleasure. Then he'd meet her back at home, where she would dictate how to proceed.

After that, there'd be no looking back. He would coax her into confessing her fears, and he would reassure her that there were ways other than complete abstinence to achieve her desires. *Their* desires.

Soon they would be as one again.

He was caught by surprise by her low, wicked laugh as she rolled onto her stomach and clawed her way on top of him, her little fingers clumsy in their haste as she grappled with the buttons of his breeches.

He could hardly believe it. Now she was straddling him, her skirt hiked up to her waist, her soft lily-white body pulsing to receive him. He tried to raise himself to cast a seeking hand for the receptacle which contained the French letter, but Cressida was now nuzzling his neck, kissing his throat. It was thrilling to be the object of her desire like this, but it was certainly no way to ensure they did not to add a sixth little angel to the nursery.

No, tonight he'd imagined a far more cautious return to sexual intimacy. With perhaps a great deal of talking and a revealing of identities to precede a gentle, pleasurable exploration of each other's bodies.

Cressida had chosen to retain the secrecy. He could not reveal that he knew her, call her by name. Yet what should he do when she was hell-bent on satisfying her extraordinary desire? She must have forgotten herself. And her fears—though if Justin wanted to reclaim such exquisite carnal pastimes on a regular basis, he could not forget himself under the onslaught of her unbridled enthusiasm.

"Wait," he ground out as he gently but firmly pushed her hand away and rose to his feet, his eyes scanning the mantelpiece. To his horror, the book in which he'd secreted the French letter he'd initially doubted he'd need tonight wasn't there. He cast around the gloom, but could not see where it had fallen. It must have happened when Cressida had been gripping the mantelpiece just seconds before.

CRESSIDA FROZE, HER FINGERS STILL BENEATH HIS HAND AS HIS protest reverberated round her fevered brain.

Uncertainty replaced desire like an arctic wind through an open doorway.

She'd come here in disguise, fully believing Justin knew exactly who she was. She had the Queen Anne's Lace seeds and had douched herself with vinegar to afford her some protection against conception. It was by no means as effective in preventing conception as a French letter, but she was prepared to take the chance, intending this moment to be the greatest gift she could give her darling husband after ten months of silent resistance to his loving overtures.

Now his words tore asunder her confident assumptions.

Justin's reluctance to consummate their sexual congress suggested he really did not recognize her or that he was in the habit of receiving strange women in Mrs. Plumb's private sitting room.

She shrank back from him. He did not want her? No, it could not be that. In which case, it could only mean that he did not know it was her. But Justin would never involve himself so wantonly with a stranger. She was too confused and uncertain to know what to say. Could he really kiss and fondle and suckle a desirable, unknown woman as long as he virtuously refrained from penetrating her so he could still guiltlessly smile at his wife over breakfast the next morning?

She could not see his face beneath his mask in the dim light, but she sensed he knew something was amiss.

"Please! Just wait a moment. I...I'm looking for something. We mustn't get carried away."

Carried away? Not wanting her reaction to strike a discordant note, she smoothed her skirts and rose with dignity while she re-buttoned the front of her dress, saying in a strained attempt at sounding jaunty, "We did get carried away but...it's late and time I left."

"Don't leave. Wait. I must find something and then we can—"

But Cressida wasn't waiting to hear more. The roar in her ears drowned out his protests as she hurried to the door, fumbling with the key in an attempt to put this, her greatest humiliation, behind her.

It was a humiliation, wasn't it? She wasn't overreacting? Overreacting at the fact her husband baulked at the final moment of consummation suggesting that tonight's frenzied *prelude* to sex was just that.

"Please, stop... We need to talk about this."

She ignored him, still too confused to know what to say. She'd exposed herself in a way she'd never believed possible, and he'd egged her on all the way, only to reject her at the end. *Revenge? Tit for tat? He really didn't know it was her?*

Oh God, she should remove her mask this minute. Reveal her identity and uncover the truth, except that Justin's reaction had been so unexpected she couldn't help but think she'd missed something gravely important and had just made herself the biggest fool ever.

"Please wait!"

Still she ignored him, blinded by hot, mortified tears as she finally turned the key.

His hand grazed her arm but she knocked it aside as he cried out, "Why come here if not to torment me? I have precautions, but we cannot proceed without them."

Dear God, so he *was* prepared to make love to a stranger, she thought wildly, pulling open the door then slamming it upon his hand so that the last sound she heard was his cry of pain.

At least that might act as a dampener in case the next available widow was only five minutes away, she thought bitterly, as she ran down the passage.

"Cressida!"

The sound of her name stopped her mid-flight, and she sagged against the wall. Squeezing shut her eyes, she dragged in a deep breath and forced reason to the fore. She looked down at her hands, balled fists, and tried to control her trembling. Justin had just called her by name. What a fool she was. Her brain had been trying to assimilate the worst-case scenario, when of course she should have known that Justin had everything under control.

He knew exactly who she was and why she was here. Somehow he'd cleverly guessed, without her telling him, that her greatest fear of intimacy was conceiving again. He'd merely wanted to halt proceedings to protect her.

Joy surged through her. She nearly wept with relief.

Of course Justin knew who she was, just as he'd known last Wednesday. He'd allowed her to proceed with her outrageous seduction at her own pace, hinting though never alluding directly to it in his loving letters of this past week to her in Bath.

Still mortified but quickly filling with hope and excitement, she waited for him to come to her, reflecting with shame upon her cool response to her darling husband's flood of correspondence while she'd been tending impossible Great-Aunt Jane. She'd been too blinded by her own fears and lack of self-confidence to read between the lines and properly interpret his letters as an attempt to reason out her confusion.

Raising her head, she smiled at him, happiness radiating through her like treacle through her veins.

"Oh, Justin, I'm so sorry—" she began as her wonderful, beloved husband strode up the passage toward her, his masquerade mask now discarded, raking his hands through his disheveled brown hair.

She put her hands up to untie her own mask, excitement mounting at the thought that in seconds, their stupid charade would be at an end and she'd be where she should have been for the past ten months—in her husband's arms. They'd waited far too long. Now, within minutes, they could be right back in that room, or, better still, in their own bed, finishing off the wonderful business that had brought them here.

As she clutched at her wildly beating heart, Cressida saw her own hopes mirrored in the expression on his face, and her heart surged with love and longing.

"Justin!"

They both turned at the cry, checked by its note of desperation, and Cressida felt her joy turn to confusion as the figure at the end of the passage ran toward her husband and Miss Mariah threw herself into Justin's arms.

"Oh, Justin!" Just two simple words but uttered in such heartfelt tones that Cressida needed to be a fool not to understand that some deep emotion bonded the two of them.

Justin did not push the woman away. He did not unclasp her fingers, which gripped him behind his neck. He did not step politely away. No, his expression changed from passion to something curiously deeper in a response that quite clearly conveyed to Cressida how much this woman meant to him. *Miss Mariah?*

"Madame Zirelli!"

She heard the name from the lips of a nearby patron who stopped in the passage and stared, confused a moment, before moving on.

Miss Mariah was *Madame Zirelli?* The woman who had been Justin's mistress before he'd married Cressida.

In the moment that the truth revealed itself, Cressida traded hope and happiness for the sorrow of all the world's betrayed women. She would have preferred anger to the heartbreak that consumed every hope for their shared future she'd ever allowed herself. What a fool she'd been to have missed what had been staring her in the face. The woman to whom Justin had turned during these long months when Cressida had not wanted him *had* indeed been his old mistress, as Catherine had insisted at the ball.

"Justin, I always knew I could rely on you!" Miss Mariah wept. Cressida's stomach roiled and she felt the bile, excoriating and bitter, burn her throat.

Apparently unaware of Cressida standing a few yards farther up the passage, Miss Mariah's limpid gaze encompassed only Justin as she clasped his shoulder, pulling him down for her kiss, her greeting revealing a depth of feeling between them that went beyond friendship.

Or anything a wife would condone.

Heaving in a wrenching breath, Cressida brushed the tears from her eyes and picked up her skirts, ignoring her husband's imploring call as she gathered speed, all but running along the corridor and out into the street where her carriage was waiting.

As she pulled in her trailing skirt, she heard his desperate cry from the top step of the portico.

"Cressida, come back!"

She rapped on the roof, signaling impatiently for the coachman to go.

"Cressida, it's not what you think. Talk to me—!"

He was at the carriage door, grasping the handle, while she gasped her anger and outrage to John the coachman in one imperative command that he obey *her* and whip up the horses. Hunched up in the carriage, numb and trembling with shock, she dared not look out through the window in case the sight of Justin, pleading and confused, staring after her in the street, caused her to weaken her resolve and turn back.

She'd accepted that Justin had a very good reason for being at

Mrs. Plumb's. No, she hadn't questioned that at all. At every turn, she'd given him the benefit of the doubt before challenging her greatest fears in order to give herself once more to him.

What a fool she was.

Justin would follow her and try to make her believe some concocted story, but right now she needed to talk matters over with someone who knew all about straying husbands.

For hadn't Justin been just like James only worse. At least James no longer *pretended* he cared for Catherine.

CHAPTER 11

The moment Catherine received her, Cressida realized her error.

For a start, the house was in darkness. She'd hoped to find her cousin up and playing cards or recently returned from an evening out and full of post-revelry cheer.

Instead, a glowering Catherine appeared at the top of the stairs, an enormous muslin cap covering her elaborately dressed hair and a shawl thrown hastily over her nightgown.

"Good Lord, Cressy, do you know what time it is?" she demanded. "Unless Justin has thrown you out, I've not the patience to listen to tales of Thomas' teething woes."

Cressida swayed at the bottom of the stairs, her anguish over recent events turning to indecision. She'd not come for a sympathetic hearing, for there was scant kindness in Catherine at the best of times, but she'd not expected such a vituperative greeting.

Oh Lord, what had possessed her to seek out Catherine? It was Justin she should be speaking to, not her viperish cousin. She was bound to Justin for life and, if he could explain his way out of this or persuade her out of her misery enough to enable her to forge ahead, a happiness only temporarily wounded was more than most wives could hope for under such circumstances.

With a brittle smile, she dropped her hand from the newel post and turned back to the front door, saying over her shoulder, "I beg your pardon, Catherine, and apologies for disturbing you. I've decided to return home after all."

Gathering up her skirts, she prepared to make her exit, unable to shake the image of the woman she'd considered her friend, cozily making up to her husband at Mrs. Plumb's.

She could forgive Justin. She *must*...

For a moment, she thought she was going to be sick and doubled over.

"Cressy, stop!" Catherine seemed only then to take in the extraordinarily daring cut of Cressida's gown, for her eyes widened then gleamed as Cressida turned. Then gasped at the sound of a vehicle drawing up in apparent haste by the front door before heavy footsteps sounded.

"My, my, Cressy, love...marital dramas!" Her cousin hastened down the stairs and took her arm, leading her back from the door. "You've come to the right place. I apologize for my rude welcome, but I'm never at my best when my slumber is disturbed."

"Then I shan't continue to disturb you," Cressida said, dignified while she prepared for Justin's entrance. At least he'd valued her sufficiently to make coming after his wife his priority.

Even if Cressida's recollections of the familiarity between her husband and Madame Zirelli—who had known each other *intimately* before Cressida had even met her husband—continued to make her feel ill.

She clenched her teeth. Not only had she been deceived, but she'd been made a laughing stock, and by a woman she'd trusted. It only proved how naïve and credulous she was.

When she opened her eyes again, Catherine was hustling her into the drawing room, leaving the butler to attend to the pounding on the door.

"I made a mistake. I must go to Justin." Cressida tried to pull away, but her cousin held her firmly, pushing her down onto the Egyptian sofa and adopting an attitude of the greatest solidarity as she positioned herself close, her arm about Cressida's shoulders.

"So I was right?" The edge of prurient interest was greater than the sympathy for which Catherine obviously strove as she pursed her mouth and patted Cressida's knee, saying, "My poor love, I thought you were the lucky one, and that nothing could touch the magic that seemed all too apparent between you and Justin. Now you see he's like all the rest, and you have to learn that sorrow is a woman's lifelong companion."

Her words were cut short by the drawing room door being thrown open over the whispered admonitions of Catherine's butler that Justin wait to be announced.

"Evening, Catherine. I'd like to see my wife, alone." His glance did not even encompass his wife's cousin. The tightness around his mouth and the flare in his eye as he rested his gaze upon Cressida indicated the storm raging within. These were not signs with which Cressida was familiar. Her husband was the mildest of men in the most trying of circumstances. Never had Cressida seen Justin so discomposed.

Despite the raw hurt that scored deep into her heart, there was no denying Cressida's pride at being allied to such a handsome man, or her admiration as she raked her gaze over his tall, deter-mined form. Certainly these were cosmetic, but it had always given her a thrill to know that Catherine—and others like her—envied Cressida her husband for his outward charm, good looks and obvious intelligence, in addition to his pocketbook. Catherine must indeed be curious as to the extent of Justin's manly attrib-utes, which only Cressida—well, she'd thought this until only recently—was in a position to know.

As Cressida's eyes met Justin's, the intensity of his look sent her stomach lurching. In an agony of anticipation, she watched him rake back his hair and draw in a breath...to apologize? Beg her forgiveness?

Catherine's grip on her arm dug in harder but Cressida ignored her cousin as she shifted away, staring at Justin as if seeing him for the first time. Relief had made her weak and she nearly succumbed to tears on the spot, despite the suspicion of his infidelity and the guilty knowledge of her own part in pushing him away.

But Justin wanted her. At least, he wanted her more than he wanted his old mistress, and if Cressida valued her happiness, she must show the good sense to sweep everything under the carpet and simply forgive and forget. They were bound to one another for life and, if he'd strayed, it was only because she'd denied him his marital rights for longer than any red-blooded male could reasonably be expected to survive.

She rose to go to him. Justin was her world. She belonged with him. The warmth of his gaze, his kindling look, made this clear.

As long as he didn't cast her as the credulous fool in front of Catherine, the wife who could be relied upon to turn a blind eye to future peccadilloes, she could put all this behind her.

She patted her cousin's hand, which had swooped up to stop her, whispering, "It's all right, Catherine, I'm going home with Justin, now." If there was more resignation than joy in her tone, she needed to convey her acceptance of the situation so she could simply depart. Justin's confession could wait.

Catherine thought differently. "Let Justin say what he came to say, first," she responded, gripping Cressida's skirt and pulling her down, hissing in an undertone, "Be strong, Cressy. If you meekly accept everything he tells you, he won't respect you."

Justin glared. Damn, but how could Cressida resist a man who incorporated everything her heart desired—determination, charm, good looks, a desire to see to her happiness and that of their children? She sucked in a wavering breath. If he'd strayed, he regretted the pain it had caused her. She still came first in his world. She had to believe it, or *her* world was nothing but dust.

He spoke quickly, holding out his hand before Cressida could reply and in the dim light of the candle on the mantelpiece, and the dying embers in the great, he'd never looked more appealing. "Please, Cressy, I need to speak to you alone."

Justin could always make him want her. Even now she felt her desperate need for him override every other painful emotion she'd endured during the past week. He could put her through nameless torments and she'd still want him.

The knowledge threaded its way uncomfortably through her veins.

Should she accept everything he said so meekly? Catherine was right. There came a time when, for her own survival, it was incumbent upon her to stand up for herself.

With another short, sharp tug, Catherine forced Cressida to resume her seat on the sofa beside her while she took the initiative, saying in her thin, superior voice, "Cressida came to me because she was deeply upset by recent events."

Although Catherine had had no direct confirmation that Cressida had ventured into Mrs. Plumb's sinful establishment, her words suggested a knowledge that went far deeper than any confidence with which Cressida had entrusted her.

Cressida turned to stare at her cousin. Catherine's capacity for interference suddenly frightened her. Justin would not, could not, deny the existence of Mariah Zirelli, but now was not the time for such a confession. Catherine would be like a dog with a bone. She would use Justin's guilt for her own ends. His remorse, and the torture Catherine would put him through, would go some way toward alleviating the pain caused by Catherine's own husband's painful lack of any finer feelings, but it had the potential to destroy Justin in his own eyes.

"It's all right, Catherine." Cressida stood once more, no longer desperate to hear her husband beg her forgiveness. He could do that later, without Catherine to witness it.

She was prepared for silence, even for a mumbled, "We'll talk about this later," but Justin's response struck a heavy blow to her new resolve when, in a tone almost of injury, he said, "I'm sorry to see you've been caused pain, Cressy, but you've misunderstood matters." The flinty gaze that he'd leveled upon Catherine softened as he held out his hand to Cressida. "I'm so glad to see you safely here, my darling, when I was so worried. Everything will be all right when we are alone."

Alone... Oh, how Cressida longed for it.

"So Cressida's eyes deceived her." Catherine's voice was smug. She smiled at her cousin. "I'm sure you're greatly relieved to hear that, my dear, but I think the fact you've woken me at such an ungodly hour deserves an explanation. What is the cause of your distress, which Justin is so anxious to make you believe was *nothing?*"

"It *is* nothing, but clearly Cressida thinks otherwise." In clipped tones Justin added, "Leave it, Catherine, so I might explain everything in private."

Catherine shifted, patted Cressida's arm, and said smugly, "But I have been drawn into the middle of it, haven't I? And I want an answer more satisfactory that the one with which you've fobbed off Cressida. Come Justin, if her eyes deceived her—and that's why she's so upset—what did she *see?*"

Torn, Cressida sank back into her seat, wavering, then ultimately rejecting the hand her husband extended toward her. Justin had quite clearly denied the truth of that which could not be denied. Cressida had seen him in the arms of the woman who'd been his former mistress right up to the eve of his marriage. The woman, rumor had it, to whom he'd returned. Furthermore, it was at a notorious House of Assignation.

Did Justin truly think Cressida such a gullible fool? Was she nothing more than a doormat who could be relied upon not to make a fuss and to turn a blind eye whenever he chose to stray?

Catherine was not to be denied her evening's entertainment. Ignoring Justin, she ran her hand over Cressida's black silk skirts. Her eyes glittered with curiosity. "Where *have* you come from tonight, Cressy? I can see it's not masquerade, so surely it's some wild disguise?"

"Nowhere you'd know," Cressida mumbled while she still agonized over whether she'd stay or go with Justin.

"Nowhere I'd know." Catherine repeated Cressida's words

slowly, clearly intrigued. "Why, Cressy, I didn't think you had it in you. It's Wednesday, isn't it? And if you weren't at home or with me, why surely you've been at Mrs. Plumb's? Look at you. I've never seen you look so dashing..." Her words trailed away. She tilted her head to look at Justin, and her mouth curved in a speculative smile. "But I fear something at Mrs. Plumb's has upset you. Something involving your husband and," she added, carefully, "perhaps another woman."

Justin seized Cressida's hand and pulled her to her feet. It was the ungentlest action Cressida had ever experienced at his hands and a thrill of mixed emotions flooded her. She wanted to be with him more than anything in the world right now, yet there was a grain in truth in what Catherine said.

"Cressida's eyes deceived her. She is coming home with me."

Cressida's eyes deceived her? Indignation gained the upper hand and banished Cressida's desire to meekly return home with her husband. Her eyes had certainly *not* deceived her. And while Cressida was prepared to accept a watered-down version of the truth, unless she showed some backbone, as Catherine put it, she realized in this instant that this might well be only the start of even greater sorrow.

The truth was that the time had come for her to stand up for herself.

Snatching away her hand, she challenged Justin for the first time in their married life, her voice thick with emotion, her heart pounding so hard she could barely hear her own words. "I saw you with Madame Zirelli. Did my eyes deceive me as to the"—she choked down the painful swelling in her throat—"familiarity of her greeting?"

Justin stilled. "Madame Zirelli is an old friend." He spoke carefully. Was that because he was afraid of incriminating himself? "It could not have escaped your notice, Cressida, that she is also at least ten years older than you. A woman of mature years. One whose advice I have sought in a platonic sense, and whom I am aiding in a capacity quite unrelated to...everything else."

So it had come to this? Oblivious of everything around her, Cressida stared at Justin for the first time as if he were not her husband. The eyes that generally regarded her with genial warmth were wary. Surely that must suggest—she nearly choked on her grief—guilt? The lean, handsome jaw was clenched as if he hung on her response, and his whole stance was as tense as if he were about to spring.

This was not the Justin she knew. She wanted her loving husband back. She wanted this whole nightmare to go away so she could wake up in Justin's arms feeling warm and safe like she'd done almost every morning until...

She hung her head as she finished the thought.

Until ten months ago when she'd withdrawn, physically, from him.

"Do you deny she is your mistress?" she whispered, even though to hear him confirm it would be like a lance through her heart.

"I don't know what made you think it, but Madame Zirelli is *not* my mistress."

Catherine cocked her head. "Then why were you at Mrs. Plumb's with her?"

"I heard she was your mistress before you married me," Cressida whispered.

"Yes," he said, carefully, "*before* I married you, she was my mistress."

"Then you *admit* you lied to me just now!" Cressida clapped her hand to her mouth. "Why not just tell me I forced you away? That I pushed you into the arms of this woman who could be relied upon to...give you the comfort I couldn't—"

"Good Lord, Cressy, you are overwrought!" Seizing her wrist once more, Justin pulled her to her feet. tilting her chin with his forefinger as he forced her to meet his eyes. "That is not what happened at all. I have not been unfaithful in mind or body for the entire eight years we've been married."

"Then tell me, what were you were doing at Mrs. Plumb's?"

begged Cressida. "Last week, when I saw you there for the first time, you were in her sitting room, clearly not expecting *me*. Yet when a...widow in need of manly attention came knocking, you—"

"Do you think I don't know my own wife?"

Cressida shrugged helplessly. "I don't know." Miserably, she sank down into the cushions beside Catherine when Justin released her. "I didn't know what to think, but I wanted you back, Justin." She stared at her feet. "And then when I saw you with... that other woman... I realized I knew nothing."

"Cressy, I *want* to explain everything to you. Like who she is and what she is to me. But"—he glanced at Catherine—"I want to explain when we are alone."

Catherine patted Cressida's shoulder. "All fixed," she said brightly. "You were entirely mistaken, my dear, and I'm so pleased this drama is on such shaky foundations. However, if it really is nothing more than a snowflake in a snowstorm, surely I can be privy to Justin's simple explanation as to what he was doing at Mrs. Plumb's with his apparently *former* mistress?"

"I'm sorry, Catherine, but I'm taking Cressida home to continue this conversation...in private."

The pressure of his hand on Cressida's shoulder was enough to send the blood rushing to her head, demonstrating yet again that she had no resistance against him.

"If you have no secrets, I wonder why you won't reveal why you were at Mrs. Plumb's at all?" Catherine asked sweetly.

Justin stared down at them, his face an inscrutable mask. No hesitation as to what he was about to do, or regret as to what he had done, crossed his handsome, normally mobile features.

With a curt nod at Catherine, he muttered, "You are a dangerous woman, Catherine, but sadly, you have not a care for the hurt you cause your cousin."

Cressida was half on her feet, but her obvious wavering was too much for him. Before she had a chance to make her decision, Justin bowed, then turned on his heel and left.

CHAPTER 12

For two hours, Catherine had ranted over a husband's inability to remain faithful to his wife and about a wife's duty for the sake of womanhood to punish him for his failings.

For more than twenty years, she'd bullied Cressida, making her cousin feel small and insignificant. Cressida was too small of stature to command the respect the tall—now gaunt- looking—Catherine received as her due. Cressida's nose was too small for her little face, though the long shadows cast by the dim firelight tonight turned Catherine's into a hawk- like proboscis wedged between the hard angles of her cheeks.

Catherine had implied that by extraordinary good fortune, Cressida had snared a jaded noble on the rebound, although in the happy years that had followed their marriage, Cressida had been able to dismiss Catherine's jibes.

Yet here Cressida now was, cowering on the Egyptian sofa beside her bullying cousin, having just dismissed her ever-patient, ever-loving husband when any decent wife would have heard him out and any loving wife would have perhaps gone further than that. Instead Cressida had allowed Catherine to hold her hostage in her drawing room in an attempt to poison her mind against Justin.

How had she allowed Catherine to assume her former pre-marriage position of such power over her? Cressida wondered as the clock in the passage struck three. What kind of wife did it make her if she couldn't even give her husband an honest hearing?

As the final chime faded into silence, Catherine exhaled on a gusty sigh and turned back from the fire. The lines of her face were pulled taut with the disdain now ingrained in her character. Why had Cressida not noticed it before? Catherine's dissatisfaction with life was poisoning her from within and her remedy was to make everyone else as miserable as she was.

She looked twenty years older than she had last week, twenty years older than Cressida, who had been born in the same year. Bitterness had sucked her dry, and Cressida realized in that moment what happened to women who could not, or would not, forgive. Women who wouldn't even give their husbands a hearing, much less a little of the kindness they were forced to seek elsewhere.

Like a dog with a bone, Catherine kept chewing. "Really, Cressida, I don't know how you can even contemplate forgiving your husband's disgraceful behavior. He was at Mrs. Plumb's for goodness' sake. His conduct is deplorable. When will you learn to trust your instincts?"

When will you learn to trust your instincts? Had Catherine really asked her that? Like a virtuous virago desperate to sink her teeth into another juicy victim, mauling Cressida and Justin at each other's expense? Rage burned slowly through her veins, filling her with the fire and fortitude she needed to make her own decisions against a formidable opponent.

Before Catherine could take a breath to launch further into her theme, Cressida decided she'd heard enough. With quiet majesty, she smoothed her skirts and rose. "Actually, Catherine, I *am* going to finally trust my instincts," she said in clipped tones, enough at odds with her character to make Catherine raise her eyebrows.

"I've had enough of your hectoring for one night. Actually, for a lifetime." She straightened her décolletage in the looking glass above the mantelpiece, pinching her cheeks to heighten the color. Businesslike, she said, "My poor coachman will have to be roused so I can return to find Justin and let him tell me what he was doing at Mrs. Plumb's before I tell him my side of our little domestic drama of the past ten months."

"Justin? How can you believe a word of what he says?" Catherine looked mightily put out at her uncharacteristic determination, Cressida noted as she glanced at her cousin's reflection in the mirror.

She heard Catherine rise and her footsteps across the floor. Her voice was closer and the tone no less carping. "You heard the way Justin lied to you, Cressy, telling you your eyes deceived you when you know very well what you saw."

"What I saw does not confirm Justin was unfaithful." Cressida continued to make those subtle but important improvements to her appearance in front of the looking glass, enjoying the novelty of Catherine's helplessness to stop her from leaving. "What's more," she added crisply as she tucked a curl behind one ear, "if he was unfaithful, I now know what I intend to do about it."

"That's the spirit." But Catherine sounded uncertain as she watched Cressida continue to preen. And when Cressida turned back to her after plumping up her breasts and tugging at her black lace-edged décolletage, Catherine was frowning.

Cressida smiled. "First I intend telling him how sorry I am not to have known how to tell him of my fears of conceiving another child."

"Cressida—!"

"Then I intend to inform him that I've now resolved those fears and am ready to be the good wife he once loved—no, *enjoyed* —so much." Cressida slanted a wickedly suggestive glance at her cousin. "He will soon be in no doubt as to where my affection and loyalty lie."

She stroked her hands over her belly and breasts in a gesture

Catherine had probably not seen before, and the shock on her cousin's face made Cressida laugh.

This night had been the most extraordinary of her life. Her encounter with Justin at Madame Plumb's—truncated though it had been—had reminded her of the physical pleasures she'd so missed. When she was in Justin's arms and the first difficult words had been said, she knew the rest would be easy. A man didn't change character overnight and if Justin had strayed, Cressida was confident enough of winning him back, now and for the future, that she was prepared to put the past behind them.

"I am sorry for your unhappiness, Catherine, but we reap what we sow. When did you last please your husband, Catherine?" she asked. She began to count on her fingers. "Let me think, your two sons were born less than a year apart. Baby William, your second son and final child, was born four years ago. Once you'd provided James with two sons, you felt you'd done your duty, didn't you? You've denied James access to your bed ever since, yet you blame him for seeking his pleasures elsewhere?"

"How...dare...you."

For once, Cressida felt no fear in the face of Catherine's anger. She shrugged. "I'm sure I'm not the only one who's speculated that. Of course, it *is* only speculation, but I'm not the innocent I was, Catherine." Excitement bubbled inside her at the thought of what lay ahead. Taking another quick look at herself in the looking glass, she dragged down the lace-edged black silk at her décolletage, enjoying the fact that her behavior was, for once, scandalizing her cousin. She swung back to face her, not hiding her pleasure at the prospect of seeing Justin again. "You see, Catherine, I realize how lucky I am. I've enjoyed a love most women never experience, and I'm not about to squander the opportunity to take it in a new and *exciting* direction." She raised her eyes heavenward and said in an adrenaline-fuelled rush, "I went to Mrs. Plumb's last week and again this week, Catherine, and I've seen things you'd not believe." If she sounded like a schoolroom miss, she didn't care, especially as she saw the effect her admission had on Catherine.

Yet all her cousin could manage was, "Oh, Cressida!" as she took a step forward, no doubt prepared to stop Cressida physically from leaving.

"So now that I am weary to the bone of listening to you tell me how to make my marriage as miserable as yours," Cressida went on, "I am leaving this very minute to go back to Justin." She gave Catherine a challenging look. "And to show him what a loving wife he has, now that I have power like no mother, aunt, sister or *cousin* ever told me was possible."

Catherine took a very slow, deep breath and a measured step toward Cressida, who was now halfway to the door. Her lips were a thin line in her gaunt, bitter face, like a smear of plum juice over a piece of grey leather.

"You'd do better collaring Madame Zirelli and forcing her to admit everything," she hissed.

Cressida cocked her head as she contemplated the idea, one hand on the bell rope. "The trouble with you, Catherine, is that you always believe the worst. Someone is always to *blame*. Except you, of course. I used to pity you, married to philandering James." She sighed. "Now I pity James. But, yes—why not? I *will* take your advice and pay a call on Madame Zirelli, despite the late hour. I'm dressed for the occasion, after all, and Wednesday nights at Mrs. Plumb's are always most intriguing."

CHAPTER 13

Madame Zirelli had long since retired to her bed, but in her dimly lit little sitting room she graciously—and with little surprise—received her visitor. She'd thrown a thick paisley shawl over her nightgown, and now in her muslin nightcap with her dark hair braided over one shoulder, she looked very kind and motherly and very different from Catherine —or any kind of mistress.

"I thought—no, hoped—I'd see you before the night was through," she said as she knelt by the grate to build up the fire. "I gather you've been held hostage by your ghastly cousin. At least, that's how Justin described her."

Cressida took the seat Madame Zirelli waved her into, and considered the woman whom Catherine would have her believe was the great threat that stood between her and her husband. Madame Zirelli might once have been Justin's mistress, but regardless of whether she now was or not, the real barrier in Cressida's marriage, Cressida realized, was not just her own ignorance but her lack of courage.

It was strange, but the truth was, she felt more at home with this woman in these surroundings than she had when she'd been with Catherine.

With a modest fire sending out a weak heat, her hostess eased herself into a chair opposite Cressida, clasped her hands in her lap and said, "I gather you've come to me for help and information, just as three weeks ago, I sought help and information from Justin. Information which he supplied and which tonight has brought me both joy and sorrow." Her enigmatic smile brought mystery and youthful beauty to her face. She sighed and leaned back in her chair, regarding Cressida with interest. "So you see, it has been a momentous night for both of us. Do not apologize for disturbing my slumber, for I've been unable to sleep, on both your account and mine. I did so hope you'd come," she repeated, adding with renewed energy, "for Justin's sake."

"Justin's sake?" Cressida bit her lip, accepting now that she was about to be severely shamed. "Please tell me," she asked softly, "why Justin was here?"

When she found the courage to meet the woman's eye, she saw only concern.

"You do know I was his mistress before he met you?"

Cressida nodded and twined her fingers together, a sudden fear overlaying her previous acceptance. She *could* forgive Justin, she told herself. She just wanted to hear the truth. Softly, and awkwardly, she admitted, "I thought he'd returned to you when he found so little love from his wife at home." She felt the color tickle her cheeks as she amended, "I mean, of the bedroom variety. I've always loved Justin and hoped he'd know it."

Madame Zirelli smiled. She looked tired and careworn yet sympathetic. And motherly. "Of course you'd have assumed the worst. I should have insisted Justin acquaint you with the nature of the business with which I charged him for fear of such a scenario as has played out tonight." She raised her hands, palms outward in that peculiarly expressive Gallic gesture, adding, "but I was afraid you'd inadvertently reveal it to your cousin Catherine, or to Mrs.

Luscombe, who are both on the board of the Sedleywich Home for Orphans."

"The Sedleywich Home for Orphans?" Cressida repeated. This was an odd departure for the conversation, and seemed not at all related to this evening's dramas.

"It was because I'd just learned Justin was on the board that I contacted him," the other woman said. "That's what started all this. I wanted information." She glanced about her, then spying the brandy decanter, rose and poured them each a glass. "A panacea in difficult times," she said with a sigh as she handed one to Cressida. She took a sip and for a moment was silent as she stared at a painting above Cressida's right shoulder. Then, returning to her chair, added in a brisker tone, "You must know that until three weeks ago I'd not seen Justin for eight years." She sank into her chair. " Nor did I intend to rekindle our friendship. That is, until a shock sighting of a young woman whose distinctive looks convinced me I was looking at my lost daughter."

"You...have a daughter?" Cressida couldn't help the shock in her tone when the basis for seeking out Madame Zirelli for information had been her supposed childlessness.

Why had she lied?

"I had a daughter many years ago but she was taken from me." A challenging look crossed Madame Zirelli's face, quickly swept away by sorrow. "You do understand under what circumstances these things happen, naturally?"

Of course Cressida did. Madame would not have been in a position to keep a child born out of wedlock.

"And my husband has been helping you to locate your child?" Cressida, who'd finished her brandy rather quickly, clasped her hands together and gazed at the woman across from her, not sure what she felt. "Because Justin is patron of the Sedleywich Home for Orphans?" she clarified.

Madame Zirelli nodded. "The Sedleywich Home for Orphans was where my baby had been sent a few days after her birth. I wanted Justin to look at the records and discover for me what had indeed happened to the child. Did she still live? Was she in desperate need? Such questions have tormented me."

Cressida imagined how tormented *she'd* be if any of her children had been taken away. Cautiously, she asked, "Has he found answers?"

The other woman hesitated. "Justin has been assiduous in his task and a kind and understanding friend when I could reveal my secret and suspicions to no one else." She closed her eyes briefly. Then, sighing heavily, she said, "What you witnessed in the corridor at Madame Plumb's earlier this evening, Lady Lovett, was my gesture of gratitude toward your husband, who had just confirmed that my daughter still lives"—there was a catch in her voice as she continued—"but that, as a loving mother with her best interests at heart, I was barred from making contact with her."

Cressida's own breath hitched in her throat, her fears escalating. *Madame Zirelli had had a child years ago? Madame Zirelli had been Justin's mistress years ago.*

"Why did you tell me you had no children?" Cressida studied her trembling hands. Vague uneasiness had taken root and was fast growing into full blown suspicion. What might have motivated the woman opposite her to have kept such a secret from Cressida?

Madame Zirelli's next words banished that fear. "My daughter is eighteen years old now, and her father, Robert, was the love of my life."

Immediately, Cressida knew she'd been foolish. *Justin had been helping Madame Zirelli as an old friend, not with a vested interest.*

"I'm sorry." What else could Cressida say? She felt foolish for, surely, she should have known a practical reason existed for the relationship between Justin and his old mistress. He'd neither have sought out, nor been otherwise complicit in the kind of clandestine relationship Catherine was so keen to suggest.

Discovering the identity of Madame Zirelli's daughter was what had preoccupied Justin the past three weeks—coupled, of course, with his, no doubt, very real confusion over Cressida's erratic behavior.

A heavy silence had descended upon them. Cressida studied the woman in the glow of the fire. She looked a different person when leached of both sympathy and vibrancy, her eyes filled with such pain and sorrow, Cressida could not fail to consider their respective situations. Both had known Justin in the most intimate way. She had to acknowledge that; and yet, she felt neither disgust nor anger.

"What happened?" Cressida finally asked. It was none of her business, and yet it was very much her business when discovering the truth was the basis of what had nearly driven Justin and Cressida asunder. "If you want to tell me, I will listen."

Madame Zirelli glanced at her, then closed her eyes. "Robert was the youngest son of a well-connected family in the local village." She smiled, as if remembering happier times, opening her eyes to add, "My father had been employed as singing master to Robert's older sisters. After my mother died, he'd taken up the offer of this illustrious Englishman and so we left Spain and came to live in a quiet English village. A very different life from the one we'd known."

Cressida nodded. Madame Zirelli looked very foreign to her eyes with her raven black hair and Castilian features.

"Though I knew Robert by sight, it wasn't until I was sixteen that we spoke for the first time, after he offered me a lift in his carriage in the midst of a snowstorm." The memory transformed her face. "After that, we found many opportunities to meet. We were in love, but Robert was just nineteen. We were too young and powerless to direct our own lives so while Robert wanted to marry me, of course his father refused, while mine was furious at what he considered my trying to rise above my station." Madame Zirelli glanced at Cressida, her gaze falling to the smooth silk of Cressida's gown, to the curve of her belly, and her expression became bleak. "I tell you this to bolster the case that I was more than qualified to speak to you of the miseries we women face when we cannot control our ability to have children."

Cressida understood. How many times had her heart battled

with her fears of the consequences of succumbing to what she'd wished could be confined to an act that brought her husband and herself so close.

An act of loving intimacy that made them as one, as ordained by the church—and yet which so often meant...*more* than one.

Cressida said nothing. Oh, but she *understood*.

Madame Zirelli's voice wavered. "For the sake of my father and, I believed at the time, Robert, I was coerced into not revealing to Robert that I was carrying his child, and I was sent away. Under directions from his mother, I told Robert I was taking up a position as a governess." Her voice thickened with emotion. "Robert swore that in two years' time, when he was twenty-one and of age, he would gallop into the grounds of my employer on a great white charger and whisk me off to the nearest church to get married. He said if I loved him enough to be patient for just two years, all would be well."

Cressida bit her lip. "But all was not well. You were carrying his child."

Bitterly, Madame Zirelli responded. "Robert's mother, Lady Banks, arranged everything. I had no mother who could even tell me what to expect, much less forewarn me of the consequences of intimacy with Robert, and my father was the great family's minion." The fire crackled and a breeze rattled the windows. She took a painful breath. "For five months, I was all but imprisoned with a cottager and his wife, who gave me food and who had clearly been directed to monitor all correspondence. I wrote to Robert, begging him to help me, but I knew my letters never reached him and that his would never reach me. We were both minors and powerless against the will of his parents."

Wearily she went on. "My daughter was removed from me when she was a few days old. Once again, Lady Banks arranged everything." Her tone became bitter. "Robert's mother had great plans for the illustrious match her son would make and I was not a contender. When I returned home to nurse my father, who was now very ill—from the trauma of my disgrace, I was told—

Robert had joined his regiment on the peninsula. I never saw him again."

Cressida shook her head. She'd heard tales of heartbreak like this before, and she knew the impossibility of a single woman keeping her infant under such circumstances, yet she had to ask the question. "Why seek information about your child *now?*"

Madame Zirelli thrust out her chin. "I was told my child had died. And even though I only half believed it, I knew there was little to be gained by tormenting myself when I had no means to support myself, much less an illegitimate child?"

"Your father—?" Cressida ventured.

Madame Zirelli's eyes narrowed. "My father was very ill, but his employer graciously agreed to let him remain in the cottage they'd rented for him, on the condition all ties between us were cut. Father died three months later."

Cressida glanced at the few meager possessions around the room, contemplating a woman's vulnerability when she had no protector. Fortunate women like herself did not tend to dwell on such matters but rather to dismiss fallen women like Madame Zirelli as arbiters of their own fates, she thought guiltily.

"After struggling to support myself through my singing," Madame Zirelli resumed, "I found myself, several years later, in the power of another man. Lord Grainger was my employer, to whom I gave myself willingly and recklessly one night, which meant"— she gave a small, ironic laugh—"that I was now to bear *his* child. The thought of being forced to give up another child I could not support was intolerable. I sought the offices of a woman who apparently"—her mouth quivered as she uttered the word—"dealt with such matters. A woman whose brutal butchery nearly killed me and left me scarred and infertile. An irony, since Lord Grainger made me his wife shortly afterward, then divorced me because of my inability to provide him with an heir...compounded by his fury at learning of what I had done."

Cressida gasped.

Madame Zirelli gave an eloquent shrug. "For years, I have lived alone, accepting that my daughter was lost to me until, by chance, three months ago, I saw her. The resemblance to the Castilian side of my family was remarkable. So certain was I that I had seen my own daughter, and so horrified by the circumstances, I sought out your husband in the hope he would be able to trace her background and confirm my suspicions."

She indicated the table in the corner of the room by the window. Upon it was a small, portable writing desk. "All the answers to your questions are there," she said. "You are free to examine any correspondence...anything at all...if it will satisfy you that your husband's relationship with me has been purely on a business footing."

Cressida did not argue. The hour was late and Madame Zirelli wanted the catharsis of knowing Cressida believed in and trusted her.

"Take the whole box," Madame Zirelli directed. "There is other correspondence which little Dorcas, the maid, slips in when it arrives, and which may not be relevant, but the document prepared by your husband and various letters pertaining to the matter are all in there."

Cressida rose slowly. She'd finished her drink; she'd finished her business here, too, it seemed. All that remained was for her to verify what the other woman had said, though it seemed hardly necessary now. After such an evening during which she'd experienced every emotion from the greatest of despairs to the heights of hope, she was exhausted. She would put the box away in a cupboard and she'd embrace her husband with all the joy and hope her encounter with Madame Zirelli had fostered.

When Cressida was halfway to the door with the writing box under her arm and the interview at an end, Madame Zirelli detained her with a languid wave of her arm and a sad but encouraging smile. "Lady Lovett, your husband severed contact with me eight years ago...the very day after he first set eyes on you, in fact." Her smile was warm rather than burdened by her personal sorrow. "Few women have the power over their husbands you appear to wield. Go to him, my dear. Use the knowledge I have given you. And be happy."

᪣

CRESSIDA WAS BORNE HOME BY A VERY WEARY LOOKING JOHN the coachman and let into the house by a rather crumpled looking housemaid. She'd never been out so late on her own, but while she felt guilty, she felt not the least bit tired.

Nervous energy and anticipation bolstered her. She hurried up the stairs and, at the landing, hesitated as to whether she'd turn right to Justin's apartments or left, to hers.

She was still clutching Madame Zirelli's little writing desk. She needed to put that down somewhere. Also, she wanted to make some discreet improvements to her appearance because...

It mattered.

The details of Madame Zirelli's story were not important. Not right at this moment, because Madame Zirelli's tragedy had occurred in the past, and neither Justin nor Cressida could help her, though Justin had done what had been asked of him. Cressida was saddened and moved by the woman's sadness and grateful, too, that Madame Zirelli had shared it with Cressida in order to help her. Now it was time for Cressida to help herself. Madame Zirelli had given her the tools.

Moving the candlestick that her maid had lit from where it sat beside her bed to her dressing table, she took a seat. She'd told the girl not to wait up for her, assuming when she left for the night that Justin could perform the necessaries of undressing the lady of the house.

Though there'd been a hitch in proceedings, he still could, she thought with a fizz of exultation as she reflected on the fact that she had all the joy she could wish for ahead of her while Madame Zirelli had only a dried up future and the sorrow of discovering a daughter she could never acknowledge.

Just up the passage, Justin lay sleeping. He'd been crushed by her disloyalty earlier that evening, but Cressida had to think past that to all the ways she could atone.

Two hours ago, Madame Zirelli had seemed the incarnation of the evil that could come between a husband and a wife. Now Cressida had to acknowledge the huge debt she owed the woman.

And act on it.

Quickly and with mounting excitement, Cressida tidied her hair and dusted a discreet veil of powder over her heated face. Her body pulsed with the knowledge of the power it soon would yield. Justin had left her at Catherine's, believing she would allow herself to be swayed by her overbearing cousin.

But Cressida was stronger than that and instead of either remaining with Catherine or hurrying home, she'd sought answers from Madame Zirelli.

She'd not been disappointed.

Now, every minute that passed seemed a minute too long before she could bask in Justin's embrace and enjoy what she'd missed for so long.

A pair of hopeful eyes stared back at her from the looking glass. The dispirited, frightened creature Justin had encountered at Catherine's was nowhere in evidence.

In a burst of excitement, Cressida rose, accidentally knocking the writing desk from her dressing table with her elbow.

It crashed to the floor, breaking apart and spreading pages to the far corners of the room.

Anxious not to delay her visit to Justin a moment longer, Cressida crouched and quickly tidied the various papers, the words on numerous reports and pieces of parchment blurring before her eyes. There was no point in reading them. Perhaps she never would. Justin could discreetly return them, for Cressida understood too well now the bleak history of a woman who'd been stripped of her one true love and her child—a sorrow compounded when she'd become a victim of sexual exploitation and finally, with no family support, had nevertheless managed to carve out a life for herself against the odds.

Hurriedly, she placed the pages in the remains of the little writing desk and was about to close the lid when she noticed a single folded letter sealed with wax had fallen to her seat. When she picked it up to place it with the others, the seal disintegrated and the letter unfolded before her eyes.

She saw the name Sir Robert and, to her surprise and confusion, another name jumped out at her amidst the tight, spidery scrawl of the unfamiliar hand.

Annabelle Luscombe. Annabelle was her old friend. She was involved with the Sedleywich Home for Orphans together with Justin.

Her eyes returned to the name of the letter writer: Sir Robert?

Sir *Robert?* Surely a coincidence—and surely not the Robert of whom Madame Zirelli spoke? If it was, why would the letter be unopened? Without reading full sentences, Cressida scanned the letter and another name jumped out at her: Lady Banks.

Without thinking what she was doing might be wrong, Cressida carefully smoothed the letter, sat down upon the chair and began to read. As she moved from the familiar greeting, her confusion grew.

"My dear Mariah—" Sir Robert began.

If this *was* the same Robert, Cressida tried to remember what she knew of Sir Robert. He was married. He had children, she thought. Though his had once been a name with which she'd been familiar, she'd not heard mention of him in years.

"I do not know if this will find you, or indeed where you are or whether you are married. I was saddened at news which filtered through to me in Basle, where I've lived the past sixteen years, of your divorce, but I hope you have found the happiness you deserve.

Throughout the fifteen years of my marriage, I have thought of you with great fondness, hoping that life has treated you well. I have been living abroad, returning only recently after my dear wife, Lucille, died, and indeed I'd not have risked stirring up the past, Mariah, were it not for an occurrence some weeks ago which begs for clarification if I am ever to sleep easily again.

It is difficult for me to write this, but I have no choice for if—as I believe—I have been in ignorance these past nineteen years, then you have carried a terrible burden.

Several weeks ago, I attended Lady Sommer's ball where I chanced upon a girl who bore such an astonishing resemblance to you that I cried out to my friend, "Who is that young woman?"

"Don't you know your own niece?" he told me. "Your sister's child, Miss Madeleine Hardwicke. She is to marry Lord Slitherton in six weeks."

In the intervening sennight, I have pondered the matter and my disquiet has not abated.

Mariah, you cannot know how distressed I was at our enforced separation and the lengths to which my parents went to ensure I remained at Oxford rather than rush back to see you when I heard you'd been engaged as a governess in Dorset.

As you did not reply to my letters, I did not persist, thinking you wished to close that chapter of your life.

It is strange, returning to England after sixteen years to find both my parents dead. I know Lady Banks was no friend to you and if I could have turned back the clock to make that chapter of my life right, I would do it.

But life is full of regrets and we cannot change the past, though we can atone—and, if I could, I would.

Now, sadly, my older my older sister—whom I feel I never knew; and is the mother of a child I've never met and whom she believed she could never have—is to follow our parents to the grave. I have so many unanswered questions.

Perhaps you have some of the answers. Nothing would gladden my heart more than to meet with you again, so we may discuss all that happened so many years ago.

With fond memories,

Yours ever, Robert."

Cressida dropped the letter. Madame Zirelli's kindness toward Cressida had stemmed from a genuine wish to supply her with the knowledge to control her own fertility, because it was this lack of knowledge that had ruined her own life.

Ruined, because she'd been stripped of a child she could never know.

Tonight, Madame Zirelli had learned that Miss Madeleine Hardwicke was the daughter she could never acknowledge. In three days, Miss Hardwicke would marry the ageing peer, Lord Slitherton. How well Cressida remembered the lackluster spirits of the apparently once-vibrant young woman as she stood beside her intended at the ball that would change Cressida's life. The ball at which Catherine had stripped bare Cressida's belief in her husband.

Such lies!

Cressida refolded the single sheet of vellum and tapped the table with it, unable to dismiss the uncomfortable knowledge that the wedding would be as decidedly lacking in joy for Madame Zirelli as it would be for Miss Hardwicke. And poor Miss Hardwicke would have to live with the consequences for many unhappy years to come.

Slowly, Cressida rose, tossed back her head and studied her face in the looking glass.

She could not think of Miss Hardwicke now. Cressida had other priorities. No, poor Miss Hardwicke and her unhappy state of the heart would have to wait.

So would Madame Zirelli's.

But right here in Cressida's hands, was surely the antidote to a great deal of unhappiness.

She dropped her hands and again stared at her reflection. Her eyes shone, her cheeks glowed. She looked like a woman in love. A woman with the world at her feet.

A woman at the height of her power and beauty.

What a galvanising thought.

Stroking Madame Zirelli's little writing box, she ran over all the possibilities.

A few hours remained of the long, confusing and extraordinary night she'd just experienced.

Many years of happiness stretched ahead of her. She truly believed that.

But what of the fates of Madame Zirelli and Miss Madeleine Hardwicke? Their helplessness and their sorrow weighed heavily on Cressida's shoulders and she wished she had the means to wave a magic wand to effect their future happiness.

But...didn't she have the means to do just that?

Knowledge. She had knowledge and knowledge was power.

Pushing back her shoulders, Cressida made a vow.

She would do what she could. She would do everything in her power to persuade Justin to exert his power to do what he could to make things right.

Maybe, just maybe, Cressida thought with breathless excitement as she pinched color into her cheeks, she might be able to unite some unlikely forces and give the *ton* something to *really* get excited over.

Maybe, just maybe, she could take the initiative, for once, and not only direct her own future on an onward loving course with her husband, but do something that would advance the happiness for two other deserving, hitherto helpless, woman.

Wouldn't that be a something to celebrate?

CHAPTER 14

"Cressida?"

Justin, billiard cue in hand, jerked round as Cressida pushed open the double doors to the games room and stepped inside the heavy double doors. A nervous tic pulled at the corner of his mouth as he regarded her through black eyes shadowed within cavernous sockets.

Cressida's heart lurched. It looked like her poor darling had been pacing the house like a caged beast, tormented, since she'd apparently sided with Catherine all those hours ago.

But she'd not known, then, what she knew now.

She tried to banish her guilt with the knowledge that she was here with a very altered perspective.

And a very altered motivation.

"Justin, forgive me." She took a few steps towards him, then stopped, regarding him more closely as he stared warily at her. There was a desperation about him that was so at odds with his usual *sang froid* that struck Cressida like a blunt instrument. Justin had always seemed so in charge, able to ride out any storm.

And yet, her behaviour had clearly rocked him to the core, leaving him wounded and vulnerable.

She had done that. She had had the *power* to do that.

A power she'd abused.

"Justin, I know the truth. I know that everything you've told me is the truth and I'm here to apologise."

She didn't move forward, waiting—perhaps?—for her husband to come to her, enfold her in his arms and pour out his relief?

But of course, he didn't do that—and it was hardly surprising he did not, for hadn't Cressida led him a merry dance these last few weeks?

No, months.

Justin was in no position to know what Cressida wanted and so Cressida was going to have to tell him.

Or show him.

"Good Lord, Cressy. What are—?"

"Hush," she whispered as she wrapped her arms about him, one hand creeping downwards to undo the the buttons of his breeches.

He stiffened as she slid one hand into the slit to cup his balls gently. His instant erection, straining against her hand, sent a surge of satisfaction through her, and she raised herself on her toes to press her lips to Justin's mouth, which had pursed in surprise.

She heard him swallow. And then his voice, low and warning as he pulled slightly away, "I have not the fortitude to bear this if you don't truly mean it, Cressida."

The air left Cressida's lungs in a rush as she returned the flat of her soles to the ground. Her determination almost followed. Of course she should have prepared for such a response. Everything she'd put him through would lead to such scepticism.

She tried again.

"Please trust me, Justin. I know I've hurt you. But this...this comes from the heart," she assured him, hesitating as she weighed up whether to continue.

Or should she just stop proceedings and simply explain, in plain and straightforward terms, what had led to this?

He relaxed slightly but he didn't take this avowal with the

unadulterated pleasure that would have made her task so much easier.

Tensely, she reassessed her tactics. Her bravado. No, she couldn't simply tell him. He had to know how she *felt*. He had to feel it from the bottom of his heart. If he had to learn to trust her again, then so be it. Now was as good a place and time to start as any.

With one hand on his shoulder and the other fondling Justin's manhood, Cressida twined her arms about his neck and pressed herself close again.

At first his response was only lukewarm but as she deepened the kiss, her tongue darting inside to explore the cavern of his mouth, she registered his excitement building in tandem with her own.

He'd dropped the billiard cue and trapped her between the edge of the heavy table.

"God, Cressy, I hope you know what you're doing," he croaked between kisses, holding her as if he could never let her go.

"I do, Justin," she reassured him, slithering suddenly to her knees.

"Cressida...darling!"

Yes, this was bold. She'd done this not so long ago as a delaying tactic and in desperation, inspired by the vestal virgins; but now she was doing it because she wanted to pleasure her husband—and it didn't matter where proceedings went from there.

Gently, she eased Justin's manhood from his breeches, and weighed it in her hand. Lord! She was fascinated. So this was the power he wielded with such devastating results...under cover of darkness in the bedroom, beneath the counterpane.

With the blood pounding in her ears, she grasped her husband firmly and gently circled the tip with her tongue, thrilling to feel his whole body stiffen.

He held himself tightly as he gently stroked the top of her head. "Oh my God, Cressy, you are full of surprises." His whisper was delighted and full of awe.

Cressida raised her eyes to slant him a sly smile as she murmured, "While looking for you at Madame Plumb's, I stumbled upon a tableau not meant for the eyes of a lady." It seemed only right to hint at her journey to this point. He needed to understand something behind the change in her. "And yet I think we were all ladies at Mrs. Plumb's, and most of us were looking for the same thing."

Of course, having a chat at this juncture was not the height of amorousness but Cressida didn't want him to fear she'd leave him in the lurch at the last moment—as had happened before.

At his frown, she clarified in a low whisper, "Ways in which we might combine pleasure with power." She stroked him then, still on her knees and looking up at him, kissed him with great tenderness. "I'm so sorry for all that you've been through, Justin, but I have learned so much. And do you know who has taught me so well?"

He closed his eyes and shook his head. Perhaps he didn't want to know right now. No, of course he wouldn't. Cressida had a lot to learn on how a man behaved under the onslaught of pleasure-giving such as she was used to receiving from her husband.

But...he needed to know.

"I was looking for you, Justin, and I met a woman who was kind to me. A woman who gave me information I desperately needed but...I didn't know how to ask. She gave her name as Miss Mariah but it was only when I heard her call out to you in the corridor at Mrs Plumb's that I realised she was—" Her breath hitched in her throat and Justin, seeming to realise what she was about to say, gripped her shoulders to pull her up as Cressida finished, "Madame Zirelli."

She wriggled out of his grasp, shaking her head as she maintained her position on the floor. "No darling, this is for you. Let me do this in my own way. Just know that I now understand who and what she is: a good woman and no threat to me, as I'd feared." Putting her fingers to her lips to as she prepared to dip her head once more, she added, "Nor have I the slightest doubt about your constancy."

"Enough talking, my darling, for I know——" he growled, but whatever else he was about to say was truncated by a deep groan as she took him deeply into her mouth, sliding her tongue around the base of his engorged member, her whole body tingling with excitement, power and anticipation at his responses as she licked and suckled.

His hands tangled in her hair as he threw his head back, his face a mask of ecstasy, she was excited to see when she flicked open her eyes. "You are exquisite," he groaned, his breathing tortured as Cressida built up the tension with her tongue.

It was all so new to her, and all so wickedly exciting. She could afford to be as tantalizing as she wished, for she had precautions and she had knowledge. A week ago, this hugely important aspect of her life, the foundation of her marriage, had been mired in dark, swamp-like ignorance.

While Justin moaned his pleasure, Cressida could provide him with all he could want of a wife, fulfilling her conjugal side of the contract. With interest. Without repercussions every time. Without fear. It was exhilarating, and it was just the beginning.

"And now it's my turn," she whispered when she felt him nearly at the cusp. She wanted this moment to confirm their sexual life would never be the same but yet, oh, so much better.

Still holding him with one hand, she hastily retrieved the French letter from the reticule at her knees and slipped one of the strange sheaths Madame Zirellia had given her onto him, stroking and massaging him to keep up the momentum. Not that that seemed in any danger of slipping.

He was shocked at first, but he understood, throwing himself into the game with as much enthusiasm as she'd hoped. Her womb throbbed with want and she was desperate for him by the time she rose to her feet, twisting in his grasp so she had her back against the table.

She did not have to say the words that had been forming on her breath—'Take me here.' Her actions conveyed their own eloquence, and with a cry of pleasure, Cressida threw back her head and gasped as his hands encircled her waist and he lifted her onto the table, moving in to take her ankles and wrap her legs around him.

Breathless, panting and excited, they laughed as together they hoisted her skirts up around her waist.

She wanted no preliminaries. She was clear about that, her lust too advanced, her desire too urgent. She needed to feel herself full and hot with him thrusting deep inside her. She wanted him to lose himself in her as he'd done when they were lovers as much as newlyweds, and the consequences were a bonus, not a bane.

She wanted to reclaim him.

With her arms supporting her weight, she opened lust-laden eyelids as Justin pushed into her, first with tentative exploration, for it had been so long since they'd done this, then with serious intent as he picked up the pace with smooth assurance. She sucked in a sharp breath as she closed her eyes, thrilling at the memory of Justin's expression, glazed with passion.

It came naturally. She moved with him as he ground his hips against hers; and her mind moved on to inhabit a different plane, it seemed, while her body immersed itself in the moment, a mass of heightened sensation.

As important as the physical was the knowledge that she had claimed back what she'd thought she'd lost forever.

He came with a shudder, and she wrapped her legs even tighter around him and thrust her own body forward to clasp his head to her chest.

"My God, Cressy," he groaned, "I had no idea how much I'd missed this." He tightened his embrace, resting his cheek against hers. "And how much I feared I was losing you."

Cressida just held him, satiated and full of joy, her husband still inside her. Justin had just made love to her for the first time in ten months—and the aftermath of pleasure was not the fear and uncertainty of another pregnancy.

Instead, added to the joyful, spontaneous abandon that had characterized the early stage of their marriage was a deeper appreciation of what each meant to the other, heightened by the knowledge of the jeopardy it had been in.

"Oh, Justin, we are neither of us to blame," Cressida whispered.

They slid to the floor, embracing upon the thick wolf skin, stroking and kissing each other as renewed sexual desire quickly pushed aside post-coital lethargy.

Then suddenly Justin rose, reached across for something, and Cressida was astonished to see he held his own contraceptive between his fingers.

"This is what I planned to use at Madame Plumb's this evening," he explained as Cressida, wide-eyed, took the prophylactic from him, the wondrous sense of power growing again as she felt her husband harden at her touch.

"You came...prepared?" She felt a moment's distress. "I had no idea, Justin."

"And *I* had no idea the reason for your reluctance these past months was fear of another child." He drew her across his lap so that he was looking down at her, his eyes clouded with guilt. "If I'd only known—" He cleared his throat. "If I'd only had the mind to think beyond my own pleasure and to consider what it might be like for you to face a potential confinement each time we did this, we could have been so much happier." Gently, he stroked her face, and love and gratitude for the husband whose heart she'd been so fortunate to win swept through her. His voice gentled. "I'm so sorry for what I've put you through, when you had no one to turn to."

"Hush." She touched his lips with her forefinger. "We both should have voiced what was in our hearts, but let's not talk about that now. We're back where we should be."

He smiled as he drew her to her feet. With his hands resting gently on her shoulders, he walked her backward until she was up against the billiard table. "Now you are my captive, my sweet," he whispered with a smile as he gently stroked her bottom and flanks.

"There are a multitude of means to prevent another baby, Cressy"—he nibbled her ear, making her shiver—"and as I intend we talk candidly about our desires for each other and whether or not to increase our family, rest assured that in future you can leave *all* such related concerns to me, and I will not let you down. In the meantime, just enjoy the feeling of being loved. For indeed, you are."

"Oh Justin, I *do* love you," she whispered, cupping his chin and nuzzling his hands, which rested lightly on her shoulders, adding quickly before he closed the gap to kiss her, "I've been to a place no lady would go, but what I've learned has liberated me."

"You don't feel tainted? Shocked?"

"I have been shocked. *Very* shocked!" She closed her eyes a moment, recalling the rapture on the faces of Ariane and Wentworth, the couple whose five-year marriage could not be made public but who'd clearly found ways to bring pleasure into their union. The license they allowed each other was not something she or Justin would contemplate for a moment in their own marriage, yet could she condemn others for finding satisfaction that did not impinge on the well-being of others?

"If I had been honest with you from the start about what I was doing there, you'd have been protected from the evils that were thrown in your face."

"I'm not sure I would wish it any other way, Justin." She crinkled her nose. "For one thing, I learned from Madame Zirelli how much I love you." She paused, weighing up her words. "I also learned what a world of loving there is to be had."

When Justin raised one eyebrow, inviting elaboration, she was surprised at the wicked chuckle that escaped her lips and the unconscious ease with which she wriggled her body against him.

"Perhaps you'd like to show me?" he suggested. "We are not restricted to the positions we've already tried, you know." He fixed her with an inquiring glance. "Or perhaps you would like to take the initiative?"

Cressida started to shake her head, but his burning gaze ignited a flame of courage in her breast. Why should she not?

His breath was hot and inflammatory on her neck as she turned, emboldened by his words, pushing her bottom against his groin and gripping the billiard table. He'd pleasured her from behind earlier without consummating the act, and she'd enjoyed the sensation enormously.

"Another of your fantasies you've not divulged to me until this moment, Cressy darling?" His hands shimmied up her thighs as he raised her skirts for unfettered access, and she gasped as if experiencing his touch for the first time.

"I kept a tight rein on my fantasies, darling, when I thought of the consequences." With a shudder, she closed her eyes as his hands cupped her breasts. Instantly, her anticipation was on a par with his. She sucked in a quick breath and managed to grind out, "Your old friend has tutored me in what every mother should tutor their daughter, if she wishes happiness for her... Oh my goodness," she whispered urgently as he slid inside her.

Sweat beaded on her forehead and upper lip, and she clenched her teeth as she gripped the billiard table, her breath coming in short, staccato bursts as the tension within her grew.

Until, at last, with a gasp of rapture, Cressida's desire reached its pinnacle, her world blackened to a haze, and her body convulsed in a series of uncontrollable shudders.

Justin held her tightly as his orgasm came on the crest of hers, and together they crumpled to the floor, tight in each other's embrace and secure in the knowledge that each was where they needed to be.

৩৵৯

THEY AWOKE WITH A START AS THEY HEARD THE FIRST STIRRINGS of the servants in the basement kitchen.

"Quickly!" Justin pulled Cressida to her feet, seizing the discarded French letters, which he deposited into Cressida's reticule before buttoning himself into his breeches, smoothing his wife's tangled hair with his fingers. They ran up the back stairs to Cressida's chamber, where Cressida collapsed, laughing, onto the bed.

"Fugitives in our own home," said Justin, sliding in beside her at her invitation, still fully clad, and cradling her in his arms. Blinking rapidly, Cressida exhaled on a sigh, thinking of her long, emotional, eventful night. Justin was here by her side, where she needed him to be. She had his love and support and always would, now.

But there were others not as lucky as she. Others who'd helped her achieve such fulfilment but who were condemned by fate and penury to exist in a twilight world, shunned by the society that once embraced them. Madame Zirelli was just one. Cressida owed her friend and Justin's past mistress a huge debt of gratitude, and Cressida's sense of justice was keen. She could not shirk her responsibility. Not when the means were so within her power.

As she drifted in and out of contented slumber, she thought of the many men and women she'd rubbed shoulders with, albeit briefly, and wondered why she'd been chosen to enjoy the bounties of life. Surely she should use the power and privilege she had to help redress the balance, where she could.

AT NOON, WHEN THEY'D BOTH SLEPT OFF THE EXCESSES OF THE previous night, Cressida raised herself onto one elbow and smiled down at her husband as he stirred into wakefulness. She could hear the birds singing in the garden outside and saw through a chink in the curtain that the sun was high in the sky. What did it matter what the servants thought? It was surely better they knew their master and mistress to be in love than to have cause to whisper suspicions of anything else that certainly was not true.

"Cressy." He reached up and stroked her cheek with his forefinger. Her heart hitched as she saw the softening of his expression and thrilled to his deeply sincere admission, "I must be the luck-iest man alive."

She thought she might cry. "A loving marriage is the greatest gift a woman can hope for in this life, Justin." She tried to think of any other woman who was as happy as she, but could not. "I have you, and I realize how lucky I am in a world where so many women suffer such great unhappiness through husbands that neither love, want, nor appreciate them."

"I've always wanted you, Cressy." Justin drew her back down beside him and began to stroke her hair. "From the moment I saw you, it was love at first sight. You were so beautiful, but it was more than that. I saw such sweetness in your expression. Such kindness. I wanted to make you mine and to look after you...so that you'd be safe and protected from what can be a harsh world. I had no idea that such careful protection would lead to such happi-ness and then...ultimately to the opposite." His expression was so sincere, and his silent pleading for forgiveness so poignant she had to fight to hold back the sentimental tears.

"You are the best of husbands. You mustn't blame yourself for what I could not and did not know. But now I have Madame Zirelli to thank for making it clear to me."

He was silent, as it was clear she wanted to elaborate, and she went on, "Madame Zirelli explained so much that I needed to know, but her own sad story is a reminder that we women are completely at the mercy of forces beyond our control. Justin, what do you know of Mr. Richard Pendleton?"

"Richard Pendleton?" He frowned, as if he had no idea where such a question had sprung from, while he continued to stroke her face. "A diligent, if retiring, young man. May I ask why you wish to know?"

"Didn't you once say you thought he was marked out for great things? He's very clever, isn't he?"

Justin rolled onto his back and stared at the ceiling, looking as if he had not the slightest idea where Cressida's questioning was leading, though he continued his gentle stroking as Cressida went on, "I believe you have influence in the direction of his career? If he's so clever, why is he working in some—no doubt dark and musty—corner, living on a hundred a year, or something similar? Surely you've guessed why I'm asking you? It's because Mr. Pendleton is the man to whom Madeleine Hardwicke has lost her heart."

A look of dawning realization crossed his face, but his answer was disappointing. "Connections count for more than talent, though of course talent will generally be recognized, particularly if a young man is forceful and persistent enough."

Cressida raised herself onto one elbow. Idly, she stroked Justin's chest. It was a strong, hard chest with well-defined muscles dusted with fine, light hair, and in the aftermath of their loving, her body pulsed with the thrill of knowing this man to be hers. Snuggling up to him, she added thoughtfully, "Which clearly means Mr. Pendleton is not. Justin, Miss Madeleine Hardwicke is, as you know, Madame Zirelli's daughter, and she is to be married to Lord Slitherton next week."

"A fine catch for a girl with such a meager dowry." Justin's tone was cautious. He spoke only the truth.

"Her mother…that is, the woman who took on the role of mother…is dying and needs the comfort of seeing her daughter settled, for it is true that Miss Hardwicke cannot marry for love if there is no money to support them. But, Justin, Miss Hardwicke loves Mr. Pendleton. I saw them together last year when she was presented and so was shocked when Catherine told me she was to marry a man nearly three times her age"—she felt indignation rise —"because he can support her and Mr. Pendleton can't. Don't you see, Justin? You have the power to change that. You can pull strings, see that Mr. Pendleton receives the recognition he deserves and consequently is assured of an expectation that will enable him to offer for Miss Hardwicke."

The patience in Justin's smile as he fiddled with a lock of Cressida's hair did not have the ameliorating effect for which he obviously strove when he objected, "My dear, Miss Hardwicke is to marry in three days' time. For all your good intentions, three days is not nearly long enough to effect the necessary steps to achieve your undoubtedly well-intentioned plan. Besides which, the girl can't possibly renege at this late stage. Think of the scandal."

Cressida understood her husband's sentiment. She herself had at first not considered that Miss Hardwicke had an option when it was her family's decision to see her marriage to Lord Slitherton, with all its obvious benefits, go ahead. Now she understood the importance of making a stand for the sake of happiness.

The tone of her objection, however, was mild. "Would you condemn this poor young woman to a life of disappointment when a judicious word in someone's ear could see her as happy as...well, us?"

Justin sent her a look she'd never seen before—lust and calculation laced with a good dose of humor. With deliberate movements, he raised himself, carefully straddled her and then, when he'd caged Cressida with his body and she could feel his hot, heavy erection pushing into her stomach, he lowered his head and whispered hotly into her neck, "After last night, Cressy, you might confidently say that I'd be willing to put myself out a great deal to advance Miss Hardwicke's happiness, and the collective happiness of your entire sex."

CHAPTER 15

S ome days later, after a great deal of legwork—both in the bedroom and in the course of the duties that Justin had undertaken on Cressida's behalf—Cressida stretched luxuriously and regretfully as she heard the chime of the late hour, and sighed. "I wish we could stay in bed all day, but we have a wedding to attend."

"What time does Mary bring you your breakfast chocolate?" Justin sounded groggy, as well he might, having expended such efforts lately on Cressida's pleasure.

Without opening his eyes, he cupped her left breast then gently contoured her belly and hips.

Cressida drew in her breath at the familiar surge of sensation to her groin as she returned his hand to her breast. "My very discreet lady's maid will know by the dancing slippers I placed outside my bedchamber door that this is one morning she is *not* to bring me my customary hot chocolate."

Justin regarded her with feigned shock through one opened eye. "I should be surprised at nothing concocted by my wife, ever again," he murmured. "Now, my dear, did you not say we had a wedding to attend today?" His look was inquiring as he toyed with her nipple. "Should we perhaps concentrate on the happiness of the very fortunate Miss Hardwicke, rather than our own?"

How quickly he could whip her into a state of desperate desire. Cressida, though, was equally conscious of his erection jabbing into her thigh as he continued his languorous pleasuring of her.

"I think we should certainly make a plan to be out of bed in..." She stopped on a pause, which became a squeak as his exploration moved downwards. "Ten minutes, Justin, if Mary is to make anything passable out of my hair, which rather resembles a bird's nest after the activities of last night."

"I envy the lucky bird who makes it its home, then," Justin said, playfully. "In either of your little nests," he added, tickling her between the legs.

Cressida squealed with pleasure as Justin threw himself on top of her and captured her mouth with his.

Lord, but her husband knew how to kiss. She knew now the heavy roiling sensation she felt in her womb was not attributable to the possibility of a living creature growing inside her, but to the primal need to be joined as one with this man.

As his tongue thrust inside her mouth, the ache at the juncture of her legs became unbearable, but he seemed insensible to her wriggling, for he refrained from entering her. Did he not know what she wanted?

Finally, he dragged his mouth away long enough to rasp, "Cressy, darling, the hour is growing advanced. We should be mindful of our responsibilities, both to Miss Hardwicke and to ourselves. You know I love you too much to burden you with another little angel so soon."

"We took precautions twice last night," she reminded him, archly, "and of course, we'll do so again. Justin?"

He shook his head, sadly, as he rolled off her. "Our precautions are working overtime, and there are none that can be used right now, if you understand my meaning."

"Please, Justin," she begged hoarsely, "I want to feel you inside me. I want to make up for all that I've missed these long months."

"We'll spend a lifetime making up for that," he murmured, kissing her lingeringly on the mouth. "We'll enjoy every moment we have together, because our splendid union has been blessed in a way few others are, my darling."

She caressed his smooth cheek with her fingertip, which she then laid gently upon his lip. "We conquered what kept us apart by bringing it into the open."

"And we learned it was nothing more than fear. So insubstantial—"

"When words and *this* can heal all the hurt." Cressida finished her sentence with energy before she shimmied down beneath the bedcovers, clearly catching him by surprise, judging by his response as she took him into her mouth.

"You do like it, don't you?" she demanded, coming up for breath, and was more than reassured by his groan, though before too long, he was once more on top of her, grinding out through clenched teeth, "You don't know what you do to me, Cressy, my darling. Right now I could refuse you nothing."

Supporting his weight on his forearms, he raised himself above her and looked down, his expression grave and deeply reverential, and in the brief silence, she felt her brain and body swirl with love and longing before craving for the physical held sway, and she arched her pelvis up to meet his.

"Then come to me, Justin," she whispered, closing her eyes, for now she had the comfort of knowing there were a variety of ways to reduce the risks of pregnancy, and that was good enough for her. "I want to feel you inside me. I want to revel in you as you revel in me. I'm not afraid like I was before. I know so much more and you can withdraw. Oh—"

For without further preliminaries, he had taken her at her word, and in an instant her body was filled with him as her world was once again dominated by the man who'd stolen her heart so many years before.

It was a more gentle possession than the passionate couplings of the previous nights. Gentle, thorough, intense and deeply erotic as he thrust into her, his movements in tandem with his tongue, leaving her gasping, exulting in the exhaustion that came from the energy expended in loving him.

Every nerve ending quivered at the contact as she thrilled at the now familiar but so deeply missed feeling that began at her toes and spread its all-encompassing wave of sensation up throughout her body before engulfing her in ecstasy. Only her husband had this power over her, and she gladly offered him everything she had to give.

Her climax was deep and intense, racking her with shudders as he withdrew upon a groan to spill his seed beside her.

No, there would be no little angels joining their siblings in the nursery for a while, though, should it happen by chance, Cressida felt strong enough to embrace a timely addition. The control and responsibility Justin shared with her and the reinforcement of his love were her reward for the pain that had gone before.

❧

JUSTIN WAS WAITING AT THE FOOT OF THE STAIRS WHEN Cressida emerged wearing a fashionable gown of primrose lustring beneath a white fur-edged pelisse.

"Good morning, king of husbands," she said softly.

"Good morning, queen of wives," he murmured, holding out his hand and indicating the open door with a flourish. "Shall we go? I believe the time has come to show our support of the love match—a great institution, for all that I was skeptical of the merits of succeeding with your little scheme when I anticipated the damage to the reputations involved occasioned by the advanced timing. I am surprised Lord Slitherton was so easily appeased when it is well known Mrs. Hardwicke could not have offered anything in the way of financial or meritorious recompense."

Cressida looked sly as they descended the steps to their waiting carriage. "Then you clearly are unaware of the efforts I expended with a certain co-conspirator behind the scenes to ensure that matters of the heart would prevail." She put her hand on Justin's sleeve to explain. "There's something about happiness that makes one want to see it enjoyed by the whole world, when one's been blessed by it, oneself."

"A co-conspirator?" He looked intrigued. "Catherine?"

Cressida laughed as the footman handed her up, and Justin joined her inside the carriage. "Now you're being ridiculous. However, I am rather buoyed up by my success with regard to Miss Hardwick and Mr. Pendleton." She chewed her lip thoughtfully. "Don't put it past my abilities that I might yet see Catherine bask in the glow of mutual love and adoration. I'll have her eating out of my hand, one day."

"Just as you've had me eating out of yours since the day I set eyes on you." He leaned across and chucked her under the chin as the coachman cracked the whip and they lurched forward.

Cressida returned his smile, her heart filling with happiness as she watched the playful glint in his eye be replaced by admiration. "Isn't there a wealth of surprises hiding behind the innocent visage you present to the world, Cressy? By God, I'm a lucky man, and you know I could refuse you nothing."

His voice had lowered to a suggestive growl by the end of this statement, and Cressida, still glowing, seized the unexpected opportunity. "If you truly mean that, my darling," she said earnestly, "there are a few matters I would urge you to take up."

Justin looked so concerned at this that Cressida giggled. "Oh, nothing to do with your quite extraordinary prowess in the bedroom," she replied throatily, feeling ridiculously naughty for voicing such things aloud, even though they were cocooned in a moving carriage with no possibility of being overheard. On a more serious note, she went on, "It's about the girls I met at Mrs. Plumb's—"

"Please don't talk about the experiences you were subjected to on account of my dereliction of duty—"

It was Cressida's turn to cut him off. "You don't understand,

Justin. It was the most liberating experience of my life. Well, almost," she amended with a knowing smile. "The *outcome* of what occurred as a result of our association with Madame Zirelli was the most liberating experience of my life, but meeting the young women who worked there and learning of the sad and terrible events which had led them to Madame Plumb's is something I can never forget. I feel that something must be done about it."

Justin sighed and took her hand. "You wish for the impossible, Cressida dearest. I, too, share your outrage on their behalf. Truly I do. But it will take a hundred years to change attitudes toward these women who have, through no fault of their own, become society's detritus."

"Through no fault of their own, that's correct, Justin." She pushed her shoulders back and removed her hand, prepared to do battle, so strongly did she feel. "However, their falls from grace are generally as a result of a *man* who can behave with impunity!"

"Not all men believe they have that right, Cressy," Justin soothed.

"Of course not, Justin, and aren't you living proof?" She touched his cheek and smiled. "However, you are in a position to help some of these women. I met four of them at Mrs. Plumb's. One was a parson's daughter. Yes, can you believe it! A parson's daughter, just as I am. She became separated from her godmother during her first visit to capital and was tricked by an evil old woman who...used her for her own ends. Now this poor parson's daughter can only hope her parents believe her dead as her fate would appear—in their eyes —worse than death. She can never go back for the shame, she believes, will kill them." She drew in a shuddering breath. "Tell me, Justin, is that right? Is it the fault of this country girl who knew nothing of London's wicked ways and was tricked when she was barely out of the schoolroom? Is it right she can never go home because of the scandal it would occasion her parents?"

"Of course not, my dear—"

"And then there was an innkeeper's daughter who'd married a

gentleman who'd be disinherited if his marriage were to be discovered before he was five-and-twenty. She keeps body and soul together by dancing at Mrs. Plumb's and must continue to do so until he is of age. Is that right?"

"Please, listen to me, Cressida..." Justin gripped both of Cressida's hands tightly and gave them a squeeze.

Cressida, who'd opened her mouth to continue, exhaled, and let him speak.

"We are off to attend a wedding. A joyous occasion and one for which you can take almost full credit." His lips quirked in a wry smile. "Though I'd like to imagine I played a small role."

Cressida returned the pressure of his hands and nodded. "More than that, Justin."

"Thank you. Admittedly, it was through more than a little cajoling on your behalf, but the fact is, you made me see that rattling society's sensibilities does not always lead to a negative result, as I'd believed."

"Exactly, Justin. And I tried to tell you—"

"Indeed you did, and you were quite right."

Cressida waited, her heart beating almost painfully.

"You also taught me that regardless of society's prevailing attitudes, the changes one individual can make for advancing the happiness of even one single person makes the effort more than worthwhile."

Cressida bit her lip. Smiling tensely she asked, "So advancing Miss Hardwicke's happiness isn't the last time you're prepared to... rattle society's sensibilities?"

Justin cocked his head, then raised his eyes heavenward. "Lord, Cressida, haven't I already said I can refuse you nothing?"

Cressida covered her face with her hands and shivered with hopeful resolve as she thought of the terrible plights of the four Vestal Virgins and of how much she'd like to see their collective happiness advanced.

"Thank you, Justin," she murmured, dropping her hands to smile up at her husband. A smile with an edge of devilry. Snapping open her fan, she fluttered her eyelashes over the top of its ivory tips. "Just know, my darling," she whispered throatily, "that I'm prepared to go to great lengths to repay you for your efforts."

⚜

WELL-WISHERS CHEERED THE BRIDE AND GROOM AS THEY stepped out of St Mary's. The turnout might have been sparser on account of a bridegroom less well connected than his predecessor, but the joy reflected on the faces of the bridal couple showed nothing but their own happiness.

Their closest kin had not abandoned them, nor had Miss Hardwicke's fears been realized, that following her heart's desire would shorten her mother's life. In fact, rumor had it that Mrs. Hardwicke had rallied on account of the sudden support of her younger brother, Sir Robert, and his unexpected largesse in providing his niece with a handsome dowry.

Justin clasped Cressida's hand and squeezed it briefly as several children cast rose petals from their rush baskets at the now serenely smiling bride and the grinning bridegroom, his unfettered pleasure a welcome contrast to the bemused diffidence he'd shown barely a week ago when informing Cressida and Justin that his suit had been accepted. The intensely shy and quiet young man had been all but dragged out of his lodgings by Justin and his landlady, the redoubtable Mrs. Sminks, to beg his love to take a chance on the promise of his imminent elevation and renege on her contract with the bridegroom for whom she felt nothing but abhorrence. Miss Hardwicke had been due to wed Lord Slitherton within days and, although the strength of her feelings for Mr. Pendleton had been in no doubt, it had taken some persuasion to convince her that she was not going to be, indirectly, the death of her ailing mama.

Cressida considered herself justly proud of the current state of affairs and so felt a surge of pleasure and gratification when she caught sight of Madame Zirelli. Her former benefactress had brought tears to the eyes of the congregation with her pure, sweet voice in church earlier. Now the brilliant sunshine that sliced through the lowering sky illuminated the rawness of Madame Zirelli's feelings as she raised her head to peer past Annabelle Luscombe's rose-trimmed bonnet in order to observe the daughter she'd lost all those years ago standing on the church steps with her new husband.

Sheathed in a fashionable gown of iris blue silk with opaque sleeves and a fetching bonnet adorned with tumbling roses, Madame Zirelli was a striking figure as she stood a little distance from the crowd.

The handsome gentleman who joined her appeared to think so too, remarked Cressida, pointing him out to Justin. Tall and distinguished looking, Sir Robert said something that caused his companion to jerk up her head and clasp her hand to her mouth.

A rustle of silk and the scent of musk made Cressida turn as a familiar voice murmured, "Word has it that Sir Robert is in the market for a wife and, by the cunning look on her face, the hired entertainment imagines she's in the running." The scorn in Catherine's thin voice cut through Cressida like a lance. She glared as Catherine went on, "She might sing like a nightingale, but she'll forever be tainted by Mrs. Plumb's. Naturally, I had to make it clear to as many as I could that Mrs. Plumb's Salon of Sin is where Sir Robert found his faded opera singer. I'm astonished she has the gall to mix with the invited guests."

Justin looked strangely at his wife's cousin. Catherine's mouth was pursed as if she'd eaten a lemon.

"If you consider yourself more of a lady than Madame Zirelli, I'd remind you to keep your voice down, Catherine. We are in a public square, and Madame Zirelli is an opera singer whose reputation is in no way besmirched by the fact she lodges with Mrs. Plumb." He exchanged glances with Cressida, who laughed at her cousin's shock when he added, "You may be surprised that *my old friend* Madame Zirelli is now an intimate of Cressida's. Perhaps you would be persuaded to revise your opinion of her if you were to join us for dinner next week, when we shall entertain Madame Zirelli and a selection of notables from the arts." He paused, his eyes still resting on Madame Zirelli and her companion. "I believe Sir Robert will also be on the guest list," he added.

Catherine, usually so quick with her acid rejoinders, was momentarily rendered speechless. Justin continued, "For some weeks, I attended Madame Zirelli at her lodgings at Mrs. Plumb's establishment on a legal matter, just as I'd advised her of her rights eight years earlier, with regard to her then husband Lord Grainger's ill treatment of her."

"Lately, she has advised me on other matters"—Cressida's smile was secretive as she looked first at Catherine then at her husband —"which have greatly facilitated my happiness."

Before Catherine could snap closed her gaping mouth, their attention was diverted by the collective gasp that rippled through the crowd. The bride had tossed her bouquet over her shoulder, and half a dozen young hopefuls were jostling each other with unseemly enthusiasm as it flew through the air. All eyes were on the trailing pink ribbons that secured the bouquet of white roses as it sailed in a graceful arc over the single misses at the front of the pack to land neatly in the unsuspecting Madame Zirelli's now demurely clasped hands.

Cressida, like everyone else, saw Sir Robert smile and whisper something in Madame Zirelli's ear, causing her to raise her hand to her breast and a fiery blush to stain her cheeks.

A few drops of rain caused a titter of concern, drawing attention from the clearly unworthy recipient—in the eyes of the crowd, at least—and galvanizing Mr. Pendleton into action as he ushered his bride across the cobblestones toward the waiting carriage.

Sir Robert, Cressida knew, had lent the handsome equipage to his so-called niece's husband until they were in a position to acquire a suitable conveyance. She knew, also, that his generosity had not stopped there, and that he'd decided to reside permanently in England.

As she glanced between the bride—whose naturally serious features were transformed into a picture of sheer delight—and Madame Zirelli, she could not help but note the astonishing resemblance. In their shared moment of joy, there could be no doubt that the two Castilian beauties were related, and with a spear of foreboding, Cressida glanced at Catherine, thin lipped, beside her.

It was Justin's intuitive murmur, "What does opinion matter when one is cocooned in happiness and not rejected by one's family?" which set Cressida's mind at rest and reinforced the decision never to let others, particularly Catherine, cause her to question herself.

"Loyalty is a fine trait, except when it causes unnecessary pain," Cressida remarked with a wry smile, indicating the newlyweds, weaving their way through the crowd. "Any mother would be proud to claim Miss Hardwicke for her daughter, considering how ready she was to throw away her happiness for the sake of her ailing parent."

Justin squeezed Cressida's waist. "And Mr. Pendleton's astonishing persistence in persuading his young bride of the merits of a love match with an aspiring man of the courts, over security and money, has convinced me he will go far."

Another glance in the direction of Madame Zirelli and Sir Robert made Cressida catch her breath. In the twilight of their lives, each looked as if they'd discovered the elixir of happiness. Their radiance almost eclipsed that of the newlyweds, until with a shriek the new Mrs. Pendleton was whisked into the arms of her new husband, who covered the final yards to the carriage as if he couldn't wait to escape with her.

"My congratulations, Lady Lovett," Justin said fondly, "for notching up such success in your first matchmaking venture. I shall not hesitate to recommend you."

His words were overheard by Sir Robert, engaged in conversation with Annabelle Luscombe nearby, to whom he appeared to be introducing Madame Zirelli.

"I'm a strong proponent of the love match," he remarked, turning now to smile at the three of them, "of which the happiness of my niece is clearly testament." With a discreet, barely noticeable gesture, he encompassed Madame Zirelli more fully into their circle, weighing up his next words to Cressida, whose acquaintance he'd made the week before in Annabelle's lavishly decorated drawing room. Cressida had liked him upon the instant. His contemplative manner was tempered by a propensity for quick humor, and he clearly meant to do his utmost in advancing the best interests of his dependents. "Congratulations, Lady Lovett, for your part in securing my niece's happiness. I hope, too, I might be allowed a little credit for counseling Madeleine to follow her heart." His smile broadened. "And for persuading Lord Slitherton of the advantages of knowing when to beat a graceful retreat."

Before Cressida could respond, his attention had strayed and now encompassed only his companion's shining face. "I'm also of the firm belief," he said softly, as if speaking only to Madame Zirelli, "that the opinions of others should be of no account when it comes to advancing one's own happiness."

Cressida felt a rush of emotion, clearly not shared by her cousin, as he added tenderly, "I trust the radiant Madame Zirelli shares my sentiment."

With another glance at Catherine, whose mouth had dropped open, Cressida returned the gentle pressure of her husband's hand.

Awareness of him consumed her like a living thing. It had always been thus, even when she'd been unable to bridge the divide that her fears had erected between them.

Now all was right with her world, and once again that peculiar, intimate awareness she felt whenever she was near him enveloped her heart and body like tentacles of welcome enslavement. She shifted a little and wondered if her blush revealed the aching need in her lower belly and her desire to slip away from the wedding breakfast and instead spend the afternoon in wanton abandonment, wrapped in her husband's passionate embrace.

As if concerned with removing a piece of lint from the

shoulder of her smart pelisse, Justin leaned toward Cressida. "And I'm of the firm belief," he whispered, his warm breath tickling her ear, his words spearing her with anticipation, "that, like myself, my beautiful wife, who has proved herself so surprisingly eager to make up for lost time, is more than ready to scale new heights in her search for excitement and adventure. Without fear of censure or repercussions." He touched her cheek, his look fond. "Let's get this wedding breakfast over and done with, shall we? I'd be quite happy to discuss the success of our collective efforts in advancing the happiness of human kind somewhere far cosier than the rain-spattered cobbled streets of London."

The End

OTHER BOOKS IN THE SERIES

Book 2 in the Hearts in Hiding series

With a murderer hot on her heels, becoming the greatest treasure in a bored aristocrat's collection may be Jemima's only hope of survival.

❧

Blue-stocking Jemima Percy envisioned a quiet, reclusive life of research. But the glittering world of the *demimondaine* becomes her refuge after she flees her father's murderer, an unknown, ruthless, antiquities collector who will stop at nothing to get his hands on Jemima's ground-breaking discovery.

With one honourable saviour dead on her account, Jemima can't afford to let down her guard - or lose her heart. The only way to stay safe is to trust no one.

Not even the handsome philanderer, Lord Ruthcot, who wants to make her his mistress as he secretly tries to fulfil his dead brother's final wish: to secure the safety of the vulnerable bluestocking spinster whose name he does not even know but who has vanished into thin air. An enigma who holds the key to a discovery he knows threatens her life and whose safety will guarantee his honour.

This book can be read as a standalone.

Buy here.

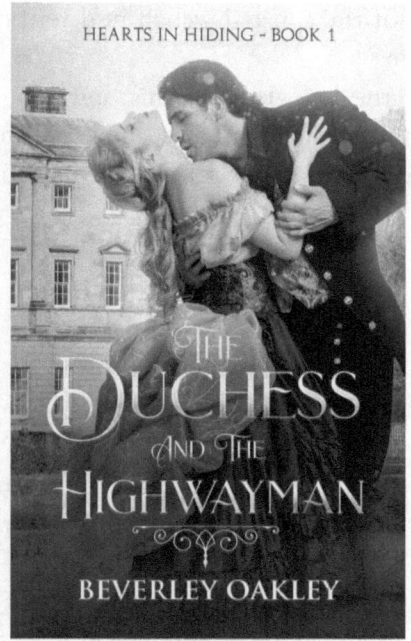

The Duchess and the Highwayman

A duchess disguised as a lady's maid; a gentleman parading as a highwayman.

She's on the run from a murderer, he's in pursuit of one.

Married off at a young age to a brutal nobleman, Phoebe, Lady Cavanaugh, longs for love—and enters into a risky affair. Framed for her husband's murder, she flees wearing only a blood-stained chemise and is rescued by a handsome 'highwayman' who believes she's Lady Cavanaugh's maidservant.

Hugh Redding has his own reasons for hunting the man whose mission is to see the infamous and elusive Murdering Duchess hanged for murder. And Phoebe, the 'maidservant with aspirations above her station' might prove the very weapon he needs—once he teaches her how to behave like a lady.

Only when Phoebe mysteriously disappears does Hugh realise

the real identity of the spirited wench he'd set out to tame—and the danger she's in.

Burdened by the knowledge of his unwitting role in placing Phoebe in mortal peril, Hugh must now polish his skills as a gentleman, not only to save Phoebe from the gallows, but to win back her heart.

What readers are saying:

"History, Murder, mayhem, lust and love, it's all there. What more could you ask for?" *- Amazon reader*

"I loved this book! It was a poignant representation of what women in the period had to go through."*- Amazon reader*

"This was the most original and different romance I have read in a very long time. Great heroine, very believable, fine hero, really nasty villlain. Hard to put down."*- Amazon reader*

Buy here

ALSO WRITING AS BEVERLEY OAKLEY

Enjoy - sizzling romance with passion and intrigue!

The Daughters of Sin series follows the intertwining lives and sibling rivalry of Lord Partington's two nobly born - and two illegitimate - daughters as they compete for love during several London Seasons.

With Hetty and Araminta both falling for men on opposing sides of a dastardly plot that is being investigated by Stephen Cranbourne, now a secret agent in the Foreign Office, there's lashings of skullduggery and intrigue bound up in the central romance.

What Readers are Saying About the Series which is now available as a complete Box Set.

"...lies, misdeeds, treachery, and romance. What an impressive story! Ms. Oakley has a unique way of telling her stories, bringing unknown heroes/ heroines into the spotlight, as they navigate a world of espionage, and intrigue, all while trying to survive and find their HEA. Magnificent and mesmerizing!" - **Amazon reader**

"Full of secrets, murders, intrigues and you feel you know the characters and want to strangle some of them, especially Araminta!!! I have since read all in the series and can't wait for Book 5... This is a series I will read again and again." ~ **Amazon reader**

Below is the order of the books:

Book 1: Her Gilded Prison

Book 2: Dangerous Gentlemen

Book 3: The Mysterious Governess Book 4: Beyond Rubies

Book 5: Lady Unveiled: The Cuckold's Conspiracy

Shy, plain Hetty was the wallflower beneath his notice...until a terrible mistake has one dangerous, delicious rake believing she's the "fair Cyprian" ordered for his pleasure. *** Shy, self-effacing Henrietta knows her place—in her dazzling older sister's shadow. She's a little brown peahen to Araminta's bird of paradise. But when Hetty mistakenly becomes embroiled in the Regency underworld, the innocent debutante finds herself shockingly compromised by the dashing, dangerous Sir Aubrey, the very gentleman her heart desires. And the man Araminta has in her cold, calculating sights. Branded an enemy of the Crown, bitter over the loss of his wife, Sir Aubrey wants only to lose himself in the warm, willing body of the young "prostitute" Hetty. As he tutors her in the art of lovemaking, Aubrey is pleased to find Hetty not only an ardent student, but a bright, witty and charming companion. Despite a spoiled Araminta plotting for a marriage offer and a powerful political enemy damaging his reputation, Aubrey may suffer the greatest betrayal at the hands of the little "concubine" who's managed to breach the stony exterior of his heart.

Two beautiful sisters – one illegitimate, the other nobly born – compete for love amidst the scandal and intrigue of a Regency London Season. Lissa Hazlett lives life in the shadows. The beautiful, illegitimate daughter of Viscount Partington earns her living as an overworked governess while her vain and spoiled half sister, Araminta, enjoys London's social whirl as its most feted debutante. When Lissa's rare talent as a portraitist brings her unexpectedly into the bosom of society – and into the midst of a scandal involving Araminta and suspected English traitor Lord Debenham – she finds an unlikely ally: charming and besotted Ralph Tunley, Lord Debenham's underpaid, enterprising secretary. Ralph can't afford to leave the employ of the villainous viscount much less keep a wife but he can help Lissa cleverly navigate a perilous web of lies that will ensure everyone gets what they deserve. THE MYSTERIOUS GOVERNESS is Book 3 in the Daughters of Sin series but can be read as a stand-alone as it features the sibling rivalry between Viscount Partington's two nobly-born and three illegitimate daughters from a completely different perspective. Heat rating: sensual. The Daughters of Sin series has been described as a Regency-set 'Dynasty'.

LADY UNVEILED: THE CUCKOLD CONSPIRACY

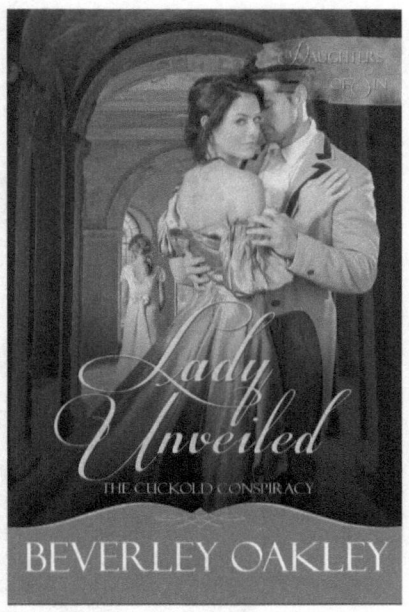

Kitty has the love of the man of her dreams but as London's most acclaimed actress and a member of the demimondaine, she accepts she can never be kind and handsome Lord Silverton's lawful wedded wife. When Kitty comes to the aid of shy, accident-prone and kind-hearted Octavia Mandelton, her sense of justice leads to her making the most difficult decision of her life: Give up the man she loves for the sake of honour. For Octavia is still betrothed to Lord Silverton who'd rescued Kitty in dramatic circumstances only weeks before. Cast adrift, Kitty joins forces with her sister, Lissa, a talented artist posing as a governess in order to bring to justice a dangerous spy, villainous Lord Debenham. Complicating matters is the fact Debenham is married to their half-sister, vain and beautiful Araminta. However, Araminta has a dark secret which only Kitty knows and which she realizes she is duty-bound to expose if she's to achieve justice and win happiness for deserving Lissa and Lissa's enterprising sweetheart, Ralph Tunley, long-suffering secretary to Lord Debenham. All seems set for a happy ending when Kitty tumbles into mortal danger. A danger from which only a truly honorable man can save her. A man like Silverton who must now make the hardest choice of his life if he's to live with his conscience.

Save when you buy the first three books here!

Save when you buy the full box set here!

ABOUT THE AUTHOR

Beverley Oakley is an Australian author who grew up in the African mountain kingdom of Lesotho, married a Norwegian bush pilot she met in Botswana's Okavango Delta, and started writing historical romances to amuse herself in the 12 countries she's lived as a 'trailing spouse' (in between working as an airborne geophysical survey operator, a teacher of English as a Second Language, and writing for her former newspaper).

Her *Scandalous Miss Brightwell* series was nominated **Best Historical Romance** by the *Australian Romance Readers Associa-*

tion. She is also the author of the popular *Daughters of Sin* series, a Regency-era 'Dynasty-style' family saga laced with intrigue.

Under her real name Beverley Eikli, she writes Africa-set romantic suspense, and psychological historical romances. *The Reluctant Bride* won Choc-Lit's **Search for an Australian Star** competition and her Regency tale of redemption *The Maid of Milan* was shortlisted in the *Top Ten Reads of 2014* at the **UK Festival of Romance**.

Beverley lives north of Melbourne (overlooking a fabulous Gothic lunatic asylum) with the same gorgeous Norwegian husband, two daughters and a rambunctious Rhodesian Ridgeback.

You can read more at www.beverleyoakley.com.

Or contact her at beverley.oakley@gmail.com.

Competitions, Books and New Releases

If you'd like to sign up to my newsletter for regular competitions (prizes include signed paperbacks and chocolate), new releases and recommended books, you can do so by visiting my website or going to https://app.convertkit.com/landing_pages/357529?v=7